ASHES FALL

A Dragon Blessed Novella

NINA WALKER

Addison & Gray Press

For Alma, Our Princess

MY FLIMSY NIGHTCLOTHES offer little comfort against the frosty air. I wince, wishing I could draw on my fire elemental for warmth, but I can't be seen up here. Lighting the darkness with an accidental spark would alert anyone who might be near. The top of our sprawling castle home is a common spot for the Dragon Blessed members of court. There is no better place to shift before taking flight. I peer around, once again checking for others, but there are none. I fear that won't last. The sky is already fading from the inky black of night to the royal blue of early morning, just before the sun rises.

I need to move.

Edging forward, the cold stone is rough against my silk slippers, reminding me that I'm closer to the edge of the roof than I've ever been before. I stare out into the landscape of the sleeping city that surrounds

Stoneshearth castle, the vast border wall that protects us, and the rolling hills beyond. It's too dark to see the mountains in the distance, even though I know they are there and I've always longed to explore them.

Can I fly? Can I really do it?

Thoughts of flight tumble around my mind: thoughts of falling, thoughts of failing, but also, thoughts of what it would be like to succeed, to soar above it all and really be free.

No more thinking. Time for action.

My dragon waits within me. I call out, beckoning her forward. She responds, ready and eager. It won't be the first time I've shifted. It won't be the second, or third, or even the tenth. But this is the first time alone, the first time I'll attempt to fly, and for that reason, I know it's going to be the most memorable. I know this deep down to the center of my being, same as my lungs know air and my heart knows blood.

This is it. Finally.

My dragon ripples outward with incredible force. She takes over my body until I am her and she is me and we are one. I blink, reptilian eyes adjusting easily to the darkness. I can see so much better than before. It's not perfect, but the mountains are now visible in the distance, sending a trill of excitement through me. When I roll out my shoulders, my wings roll with them. *Ahhh, that's nice.* I shift from leg to leg, enjoying the way my claws scrape against the weathered stone. Rippling underneath my scaly skin, the four elements pulse with magic, much stronger than when I'm in my human form. I am more me than I've ever been.

Only one thing left to do...

Flapping my wings, I lift into the sky and all my previous fears drop away. This is easy. Natural—where I'm meant to be. The air whooshing past me sounds like salvation. The weightlessness of flying feels like adventure.

It's everything I've ever wanted.

I climb higher and higher and higher until the castle is but a speck below, like a pebble in the dirt. Insignificant. All the things that were so important before, like pleasing my parents and living up to my birthright, seem minor now. As little as the pebble-sized castle.

I press forward, soaring through the cool air, toward the mountains. I have it all planned out. I'll go there, where I can hide among the thick forest and practice my elemental magic. Nobody to tell me it's not allowed. Nobody to tell me I can't. And once finished, I'll race back just in time for breakfast, shifting into my human form and sneaking into the castle with the day laborers coming in for the first shift.

The plan is full of holes. I know that. But I have to try.

I first felt my magic spark to life as a young child. My dragon slept within me, but I knew she was there. I couldn't wait for the day that I'd be able to shift, to

3

let her out and be my truest self. When that day finally came a few years ago and I shifted for the first time, it was like taking a breath of fresh air after a lifetime indoors. It was utterly brilliant—amazing!

But it all turned into a nightmare when King Titus denied me from flying or using my elemental magic. He'd gone so far as to forbid me from shifting at all, but since shifting isn't easy to control for adolescent Dragon Blessed, he had to put up with my dragon every now and then. That didn't mean it wasn't awful—experiencing the glory of shifting only to force myself back into my smaller human body has been torture. The opposite of the brilliant freedom I'm feeling now!

I fly over the pine forest, slowing down to take it in. It's so beautiful. And so different seeing it from above. The little dots of green press together atop a blanket of brown. Spotting a clearing, I land and settle into the quiet. It's darker down here under the canopy of tree branches. It's nice. Private. I'm no longer exposed and that's what matters.

I stay in my dragon form; she's a comfort I'd keep forever if I could. The elements should work in either of my forms and since this dragon-self is so underused, I can't bring myself to let her go just yet. I'm happier this way, more *myself.*

Beginning with air, I connect with the element and immediately sense it rise to life. It wants to draw the outer world in, wants me to control the wind.

Taking a deep breath, I imagine the slight night breeze picking up and swirling around me. My thought is only a thought for a brief moment before it becomes real. And the breeze that surrounds me? It's like a cyclone of magic and air and power beyond my wildest imaginings. Leaves rip through the air. Tree branches crunch against the intensity. It grows and builds, more, more, more. Panicked, I release my magic. The wind stops immediately. If dragons could laugh, I'd be laughing right now. *It worked!* And not only did it work, but it was so much easier, so much more potent, than I'd expected.

For the first time in my life, I wonder if King Titus is afraid of me—I am powerful!

I go through the other three elements, using earth to hurl clumps of rock and dirt around the clearing, calling on fire to burn a nearby bush and then pulling the water from the humid air to put it out. After that, I try mixing elements, using air and water to frost over the ground. I get so caught up in playing with the magic in all the ways I've wanted to for so long, that I lose track of time. The sky fades from dark blue to deep orange, then red, and then pink before I realize the sunrise has crept up on me. The sunlight warms my hide and casts a golden filter over the forest. I wish I could stay but I can't. Breakfast will be starting any minute.

I need to hurry back.

I gaze around one last time, taking in the mess I've

created, and shoot a dash of earth magic back into the clearing. Broken limbs repair themselves, new grass grows over what I've scorched, and the last bit of frost melts away. It's as if I've never been here.

Incredible.

A dark shape flashes between the trees, so quick I almost don't catch it. I freeze, every dragon muscle tensing. Someone or something is there. And whatever it is, it's been watching me. A low growl rumbles from my throat, and I lower onto my front legs, readying for an attack. If it's an enemy or a predator of some kind, I'm willing to fight. I know I should be afraid, but I'm not. I'm excited. What could be so foolish as to prey on an elemental dragon? To prey on me?

My eyes narrow. This could be it, my chance to prove I'm worthy to join the army.

Whatever you are, come on out and play, I think, lip curling over razor-sharp teeth. *Let's see what you've got.*

Time stretches out between the space of my heartbeats. Everything grows still.

Princess… A new voice echoes through my mind.

I jump and lose focus. The voice continues, forceful and relieved all at the same time. *There you are. Stay put!*

It's an order. And immediately I know it's not from whatever is lurking in the woods. A barrage of wings flap above and three black dragons land, surrounding me. Whatever was watching me from behind those trees is long gone.

We found her, the same voice from before calls out through the dragon telepathic link. It's a common bond we all share and I was stupid to use it before. It led them right to me. Of course the guards back at the castle figured out I was gone. Of course they sent dragons to look for me. What was I thinking? That I could get away with this?

She's in the northern woods, the dragon continues, speaking about me and not to me—a common experience for a girl such as myself. *She's fine.*

I sneer and dig my hind legs into the dirt.

She's in her dragon form. Ran away by the looks of it. All of the dragons are staring at me with jarring eyes. Their expressions suggest that they think they know me—that they think they know better. I've seen it all my life, in human form or otherwise, it doesn't matter—the condescension is always infuriating.

I didn't run away, I challenge through the link. *I was always planning to come back. I just needed a break from the castle for a while.*

A break so you can use your magic?

I don't answer that. There's no proof of magic out here. I made sure of it.

The largest of the dragons shifts, a film of sparkly red and orange energy flashing over his body before he is a young man standing before me. Dean, the oldest of the Brightcaster Princes, raises a black eyebrow at me. "You're going to have to explain this

7

little gallivant to my father," he says coolly. "I'm not going to cover for you."

I shift back to my human form as well, standing tall and folding my arms across my chest. I have to ignore the fluttering going on inside, the same fluttering I've always had when it comes to Dean. Can I help that he's utterly attractive and might one day be my husband? *No.* Can I help that I've had my eye on him for years despite my best efforts? *Also, no.*

"And you're telling me you wouldn't have done the same thing?" I ask.

Our eyes hold one another for a heated moment before he turns away with a sigh. "Let's go," he grumbles, running a hand through his dark silky hair. "It's not safe for you out here."

"And why not?" I scoff.

"Don't pretend that you're immune to our enemies—because you're not. None of us are, especially not you, Princess, with your two colored eyes. They show up even larger on your dragon than they do on this." He motions to my face with his hand like he's talking about the weather. So... factual.

Worst part? I know he's right. And more than anything, I wish he wasn't.

2

THIS IS A DISASTER. I wring my hands together in my lap, my heart thudding. How could I have been so foolish? It's hard to believe that not long ago I was flying, free and the happiest I've ever been. Using my magic, doing all the things I knew I could but haven't been allowed. And now, I'm here: somber, repri-manded, my dreams about to be squashed.

"I hope you're proud of yourself," Lady Alivia, my mother, seethes through gritted teeth. She smooths her lovely dark curls out with jittering hands and glances around our empty chamber. It won't be empty for much longer. It doesn't surprise me that she's so well put together for such an early hour. She always is. "I don't know what to do with you, Khali," she continues. "Honestly, I'm so embarrassed."

I sit up straighter and glare. "You should be on *my* side. You are my *mother!*"

9

"I *am* on your side." She sits down next to me on the tufted bench, her lavender dress widening like the spring flowers outside, and lowers her voice, "Don't you see how blessed you are? Why must you make this difficult?" She is the picture of calm, but I know underneath her practiced exterior is a whirlwind of anger and frustration.

"It's funny you should use that word," I grumble. I peer down at my own gown and groan. It's a perfect mossy green, nothing like the ripped and dirtied nightgown I'd just changed out of. That outfit is certainly ruined, but I smile a little to myself, remembering how it got that way. *I flew.* For the first time, I flew, and it was so worth it.

"What word?" Her painted lips press together, puzzled.

I shoot her an appalled look. Can she really be so blind? "Blessed." I say the word like it's a curse. For me, it's beginning to look that way.

Her face pales but she doesn't reply. I look away, gathering my emotions to be locked up inside me, and match her stoic expression. *Two can play at this game, Mother.* I have nothing more to say to her, anyway. How could I expect her to understand? She's made of more "Lady Alivia Elliot" pieces than "Mom" pieces. And besides, she's not *me*. She doesn't know. She never will. She's not *blessed*.

Dragon Blessed.

My eyes flutter closed as I remember how it felt to

be in my true form earlier, flying with the cool morning air underneath my wings. The memory brings me a moment of peace.

"If your father could see you right now," she sighs.

"Don't!" I snap, my eyes still pressed closed. Father is traveling again. It seems like he's always away, especially lately. But I know in my heart that he of all people would understand. He would not be disappointed like she's trying to imply. He gets me. She doesn't. End of story.

I try to go back to imagining what it felt like this morning, try to see it all again. I want to engrain even the tiniest details into my mind so I never forget the glorious experience.

The doors swing wide, and my eyes pop open. King Titus stomps inside. Dressed head to toe in royal purple clothing and sparkling jewels, he naturally commands any room—our family's chamber is no different. We stand and curtsy, my mother gushing what a pleasure it is to have him here and she's terribly sorry for the circumstances.

As I straighten, my eyes stay lowered, fear holding them down. But why should I be afraid? I didn't do anything wrong. I did what *anyone* lucky enough to be Dragon Blessed would do. A jolt of courage curls in my gut and I peel my eyes from the stone floor to study the man with my future in his hands. While King Titus is also Dragon Blessed, he doesn't have an ounce of sympathy for me. He never has. Judging from the sour expression on his face, today is no different. Resentment tightens my gut.

"Your Majesty." I gulp down my anger, adding nothing more.

It's only the three of us in the chamber and something about that feels more threatening than when he has his guards who usually follow him around everywhere. He tilts his head, lavender-gray eyes pinning me in place. They're framed with aging wrinkles and alive with decades of power. I swallow hard, refusing to be the first to look away.

"You were a helpless infant when I brought you and your parents here." He speaks calmly but in a gruff tone meant to intimidate. "I pulled you out of the mud and gave you a life others only dream of."

"I thought it was the Gods that brought me here," I reply, my voice dripping with cool indifference. It's a ruse. I feel *anything* but indifferent.

He scoffs. "They made you what you are, a gift to *my family*."

"They made me Dragon Blessed," I challenge.

A storm sparks in his eyes and the room darkens; the sun outside the window is quickly overcome by gathering clouds. "So you don't regret it?"

Mother reaches out to grab my hand. "She does. She's sorry!"

I rip away from her grip and stand tall. "I'm not sorry," I hiss, losing the last of my patience. "And the only thing I regret is getting caught."

Lightning flashes. Thunder cracks like a whip. The room grows cold, wind and rain crashing through the open window at the back of the chamber. Mom scurries to the furthest corner, begging the King to take pity on us. Khali didn't mean it, she says over and over. We all know what a lie that is.

King Titus stalks closer to me until he's only inches from my face. I peer up at him, my chin jutted, my stance firm.

"You cannot refuse me my birthright," I growl. Inside, my dragon rears her head, begging to be unleashed. Ever since puberty hit, she's been present more and more. If only I could let her loose right now. What would he say to me then?

"You are an insolent child." King Titus's tone is entirely disgusted. Outside, the storm of his creation continues to rage, growing more violent by the second. The castle's stone walls begin to vibrate. A tree is ripped from below and whips past our window in the cyclone of his anger. Could I do the same? Could I create a lightning storm with my elemental magic? The very idea sends a shiver of excitement up my spine.

"You think you're scaring me with this storm?" I point outside with a grin. "I'd call it a service," I continue, meaning every word. "Because if you can do this, then perhaps so can I."

The storm stops abruptly. One minute it was dark and wild and the next it's calm, the afternoon sunshine streaming in the window, an endless blue sky on the horizon. *Yeah, he's powerful.* He steps back from me, rage still eating up his face. As the King of Drakenon, and hailing from a royal family with over a century of ruling power, he's not used to people challenging him. If I was anybody else, I'd probably be executed.

But I'm nothing like anybody else. I'm Khali Elliot, the girl with two colored eyes.

That means I'm not only Dragon Blessed, but I'm the most powerful Dragon Blessed of my generation. Every time that the royals have a new set of children, specifically sons, a girl like me is born. I don't have one elemental power running through my veins; I have all four: air, earth, water, and fire. And because of that, I was brought here for a very specific reason. A reason they'll never let me forget and they'll never ever let me avoid.

"You are forbidden from shifting again," Titus says. His eyes narrow into thin slits. "You are forbidden from using any of your magic." He reaches out his hand. "Shake on it."

Shaking on anything in Drakenon seals it with magic. It would be a binding oath. I will not shake. I will only clench my hands into fists and glare at my captor.

"Now," he snaps.

Anger and worry press down on my entire being, sucking the breath from my lungs. He can't do this!

The very thought of not being my true self makes tears burn at the edges of my vision. "How is that not a monumental waste of a resource?" I ask, my voice cracking. "Couldn't you use someone like me to fight the Occultists?"

His eyes widen. "You are not here to be a warrior, or to fly, or to shift, or to train, or to use your magic, or to *fight the Occultists*," he says hastily. "You are here for the divine *honor* of marrying one of my sons and ensuring that the Brightcaster family continues to bear Dragon Blessed *elemental* children."

My chest rises and falls, but I'm frozen in place. I knew these were the rules and I certainly knew that I was brought here as an infant to grow up and become a glorified baby-maker. But to have it thrown in my face so brazenly makes me hate King Titus more than I ever thought possible.

That's how it works for a girl like me, a girl only born once in a generation. As soon as my different eyes were discovered, me and my family were taken to the castle. I've been raised alongside the royal family's children, knowing that one day the king would choose which son I am to marry. It ensures that the next line of dragon royals are powerful elemental dragon shifters. It's my birthright, as it was for Queen Brysta, and the queen before her and the queen before, dating back for ages.

I can accept that fact about my life. But being forced to squash my magic, to never shift? That's something I simply can't handle. The king could sooner cut off my leg and it would be less painful than losing my essence. I am an elemental dragon shifter!

"So that's it? After fifteen years of doing your bidding, you won't even grant me the smallest reprieve? I'm just to stay in the castle, a pretty ornament. Heaven forbid I actually claim the birthright the Gods gave me."

"Your *birthright* is to be the next Brightcaster Queen and nothing more."

"I will not shake your hand. You cannot make me." I glare. "And the binding power of such an agreement only works if I willingly agree, anyway."

He drops his meaty hand and steps back, shooting Mother a repulsed glower. "We already have enough to worry about. Do you know that the Occultists have taken control of our neighboring kingdom? The elves are being slaughtered right now as we speak."

My heart sinks. The cult of warlocks hates anyone with elemental magic. And if they've taken the Summer Fae Court, does that mean we're next? But no, we're too strong, and our borders are impossible to penetrate. At least, this is what I've always been told. But whether that's the truth or not, it's not as if I want to fly so I can have fun and be silly. I want to fly so I can fight, so I can try to help, and be myself. Why can't he see that?

The room is impossibly quiet until King Titus finally speaks again. "Lady Alivia, you and your husband would do well to keep your daughter in line, or else I might not have a place for you two in my court anymore." The threat hangs heavy in the air and Mother nods vigorously from where she's cowering in the corner. No surprises there; she's never been one to stand up for me. The king turns on us, and true to the air elemental running through his blood, storms from our chamber.

❧ 3 ❧

MY LADIES MAID, Faros, walks alongside me as we talk idly, discussing the weather and the day ahead. We don't speak of all the things I wish we could; of magic, and shifting, and all the adventures I'll never get to live out. Nor do we speak of the news that the Occultists taking over the Summer Fae Court. At this point, they've taken over all of our realm, except for our kingdom. It's the conversation whispered everywhere we go, and the conversation Faros and I don't have because she says it wouldn't be proper to talk about such things. Or maybe we think it will resolve itself on its own.

Or maybe we're cowards.

The garden path is still sodden with rain from yesterday, but I don't mind a little mud on my boots if it means I get to be outside. We've been stuck inside for weeks with all this spring rain. Not to mention how Mom has had me under lock and key since I was caught flying last month. I fight off a frustrated frown. I hate thinking about that day. But that was then, and this is now. Today is a new day. A new day, with a new plan. I'm going to prove my worth as more than just a future baby-maker, but as a powerful elemental dragon.

I will not give up. I can't.

Gleefully eyeing the rainbow of tulips that have cropped up along the winding path, I smile. The trees are beginning to bud as well, a cheerful mix of whites and purples and pinks that will soon flower. My smile falters and I swallow hard, not wanting to have to hurt one of these innocent trees with my meddling. But if I don't find a dead one soon, that's exactly what's going to happen.

Faros and I continue strolling closer and closer to the castle gate at a leisurely pace. The gate allows those authorized to go to and from the castle and into the village. Of course, I'm not authorized to leave. I peer around, desperate for my chance. On one hand, I don't want to get too close to the gate because the wrong people might see me. But on the other hand, I need to get close enough that the right people see what I'm about to do—after it's done.

My eyes dance from tree to tree, seeking the perfect one. The moment I find it, with its barren branches and sad tilt, relief washes through me. Relief that is quickly overrun by fear. Am I really going to do this? I let out a breath, nodding along to whatever Faros is saying, and steeling myself, because yes, I *am* going to do this. Not allowing a thought to deter me, I place my hand on the tree. My elemental magic jumps up to confirm what I'd hoped for. The tree is dead. The poor sapling didn't survive the winter, but maybe I can give it a proper send off and it can give me something in return.

Sparks ignite, fire bursting along its branches. Flames engulf the tree within seconds.

I yelp and jump back.

Faros's tired eyes go wide as full moons, her mouth agape. "Stand back, Khali," she says quickly, grabbing my arm and tugging me toward her. "Oh my, what on earth happened?" We exchange a worried glance and she must see something in mine because her entire face falls. She looks so much like my mother—they are related, afterall. "Did you do this?"

"It was an accident," I croak. Shame burns at the lie. I hate lying to Faros. She's only ever been good to me. As my mother's younger sister, she's not only my ladies maid, she's my aunt. She's only eight years older than me and she was brought here to be my best friend—of which she does a good job. I can trust her with most things, but she technically works for my mother, and thus, the King. She can't know about my plan. Even if she wouldn't betray me, I wouldn't want to implicate her should she be questioned.

"Hurry! We need help," I say, pulling away from

her and stumbling toward the castle gate. "I'll go this way, you go back to the castle. We need someone who can put this out before my accident burns everything else to the ground!"

It seems silly that the fire could turn large with how wet everything is this morning, but I don't give her a chance to argue. Without looking back, I sprint along the castle wall, my feet thudding on the muddy path, until I find the three castle guards standing in front of the gate. Waving my arms frantically, I scream, "Fire!" and point. Their eyebrows shoot up as they spot the rising flame and the trail of smoke above it.

"Well," I yell. "Do something!"

In a flash of shouts and panic, they're running toward the fire. Before I can talk myself out of it, I slip through the unmanned gate and out into the village beyond. I don't have much time to enact my plan.

Joyful energy crackles in the morning air, mixing with the freshness of early spring. The cobalt blue sky spreads above like a promise, little clouds of cotton dotting the horizon. I tuck the hood of my black cloak around my cheeks, sinking into the crushed velvet, hoping to hide my face in shadows. Really, I'd love to throw it off and allow my skin to soak in every last ounce of sunshine before the warmth gives in to rain yet again.

My leather boots clap against the gray cobblestone street as I make haste, little splashes of mud flicking off with each step. I'm surrounded by tall stone buildings, most built right next to each other. They're filled with life, with people—my people— though I rarely get to interact with them. Up ahead, the aroma of the farmers' market calls to me, a mix of intoxicating smells: salty, sweet, earthy, and yeasty. They're all amazing invitations to my rumbling stomach. I should have paid more attention to breakfast instead of picking at it, but as soon as I heard the newest gossip, my mind was busy dreaming up this plan to sneak out here. It's not food that I crave most anyway, though I wouldn't mind the melty flakes of a butter pastry on my tongue right about now.

I drop into the bustling crowd that inhabits the city square. The vendor booths run up and down in jagged lines, people packed into the pathways between. They mill about, pressing past me, women and men eager to get in and out and on with their day. A prickling sense of urgency ushers me forward. It won't be long until my absence from the castle is noted, if it hasn't been already. My fingers shake, knuckles aching with untapped magical energy. Perhaps it's the sunshine, or perhaps a companion to the fire, but the air elemental within is longing to make an appearance. I push it down with a forlorn sigh and take in the market. It's just as I remember: alive with smells and bright colors and endless possibilities.

I smile. I've dreamed of coming back for the last seven years.

I've only been here once before. When I was younger, I begged my mother for weeks to take me along with her until finally, on a summer day when I was nothing but an overly inquisitive eight-year-old nipping at her heels like a puppy, she conceded. While the expedition was short, I loved it. The vendors treated me like a real princess and not a prisoner—or worse, an insolent child. They offered me gifts and gushed about my beauty, telling me that they had prayed for my birth and celebrated when I arrived at the castle as an infant. But it wasn't long before a crowd gathered and a few within that crowd started yelling their angry complaints.

They were hungry. And sick.

Why wasn't the royal family doing more? Why wasn't *I* doing more? It was the first I'd *ever* heard anybody speak ill about the Brightcasters, and the shock of it stripped off a piece of my childish self— the piece that readily believed everything adults said was true. If the royals were so great, why did so many of their people suffer? Why did we live in such opulence when just outside the castle gate others lived in squalor?

Mother was quick to whisk me away from the market and that had been the end of it.

Since then, I've not been allowed to venture into the village of Stoneshearth unattended and never *ever* without a member of the royal family at my side. Some villagers might not have been afraid to voice their complaints to me, but around the royals, they held their tongues like their lives depended on it. Most likely, their lives *did* depend on it. Even though the village surrounds our castle home, sometimes it feels as if it might as well be on the other side of the world. Stoneshearth Castle is surrounded by sprawling gardens and a vast stone wall to separate us from the lower classes of the city.

But this morning, I don't have to be Khali Elliot anymore. I can be whoever I want. And who I want to be is who the Gods *made* me to be: an elemental dragon shifter. So I keep my head ducked and listen intently, searching for the clues needed to make that happen. When I heard the newest gossip early today, I knew I'd finally found my answer.

Two gangly boys about my age scurry past, elbowing each other as they race toward the other end of the market. I follow, slipping through the crowd like a ghost. The boys stop in front of what appears to be a community notice board with papers pinned to the front. They egg each other on to sign up for something posted there. I grin, knowing exactly what all the excitement is about. Today marks the day that Dragon Blessed men and women from across the kingdom can sign up to compete for a spot in the King's army. I can't believe I didn't think of this sooner! After the boys finish etching out their names and scamper off, I approach the board.

My turn.

My hands shake more than ever. My breath sticks in my throat and I don't know if I can do this. The quill dangles from the string, like a carrot on a stick, taunting me. I snatch it up and sign under the fake name I gave myself when I hatched this plan: Raven Blaze. Maybe it's a silly name. Maybe I'll be found out right away. But it's thrilling to write it, it's everything I've ever wanted—to be someone else. The quill drops and I stare, heat rising in my chest, a smile pressing at my lips. I have no idea how I'm going to pull this off without getting caught, but it's my chance to prove my abilities, to prove I'm made for more than what they think of me, and I have to take it.

4

I HURRY back to the castle gate, unsure of what madness awaits my arrival. A shoddy story pieces itself together in my mind. Should I be questioned, I'll insist that in my panic, I forgot the rules and went looking for help beyond the castle gates. It's not a very good lie, but it's the best I've got given the circumstances.

I rush down the maze of cobbled streets, stone and thatched buildings flying by in a blur, and I can't help but smile. It won't be long until I'll be on that vast field of green beyond the city walls, battling for my worth. And I'll win. I'll win the tournament for all to see. Then what will the King have to say for himself? He'll have no choice but to give me a place in his army. I can still fulfill my other duties, of course, but I can be used for more than what my blood can do for one of his sons.

It's not every day someone has an element dancing through her blood, let alone all four. Each generation has plenty of Dragon Blessed born throughout the kingdom, but few have an elemental paired with it, so it would be a shame to waste my magic on nothing but child rearing. The Gods put me here to keep the royal line strong, to bring more magicked children into our world, but they must have also put me here to fight our greatest enemies: The Sovereign Occultists.

The horrible cult of warlocks are bent on taking over the entire realm of Eridas. Now that they've moved in on the Fae courts, they're hunting down anyone with royal blood, killing them all without mercy. Of course I know what the king confessed to Mother and me when he lectured me about flying, but since then I've been careful to stay quiet and keep my ears open. People think we're next, but not if I have anything to say about it. I could fight if only the king would let me train and become strong enough to beat them.

King Titus is a fool. What's the point of keeping my womb safe for his future grandchildren if the Occultist take over Drakenon? I'll be slaughtered along with the rest of his family. If only he fully understood what it is to be me, he'd understand why I need to be myself like I need to breathe. I'm drowning and I have no choice but to fight for oxygen.

"Get out of here!" A gruff voice pierces my thoughts and I turn, heart hammering. At first I think I've been caught, but then I see a scrawny boy in tattered clothing scrambling back from a nearby food stand. "No scraps for you today, boy!" the vendor yells down at him.

I stop in my tracks, momentarily aghast by the terrible state of the child. Sweat and grime is marred across his gaunt face in a way that can only mean he's either homeless or close to it. He can't be more than six or seven-years-old, and I thought I knew what a starving child would look like but this... it's too much. Along with my inner voice, it's my mother I hear, telling me how blessed I've been.

When I catch sight of his deep brown eyes, I smile and hold his gaze. "What would you like to eat?" I keep my tone light, even though it shakes. "I'll get it for you."

His eyes flick back toward the vendor.

The vendor is a surly man with a pudgy belly and a chronic frown. "Come on, Lady, you don't need to feed that little rat. He's not your problem."

"And you've made it clear he's not yours either," I snap. He grumbles to himself and returns to his cart. It's piled high with hand pies, and the scent of butter, spiced beef, and berries is enough to make my mouth water. But I'll be damned to give this vile beast one cent.

I turn away and focus back on the child. "Forget

this cretin and his stale pies," I whisper. "What else do you like?"

The boy's smile flickers but he stays silent.

"It's okay," I prod, sweeping my hand out toward the other vendors. "There's a lot to choose from, I know."

Finally, the child lifts his hand and points to another seller. The cart is selling meat and vegetable kabobs.

"How many are in your family?" I ask.

Another smile.

Ten minutes later, we've piled a basket with five pork kabobs, two loaves of bread, a hefty block of cheese, and a handful of apples. "Can you carry this on your own? Or would you like me to walk you home?"

The boy hasn't said one word, only smiled and pointed a few times. I can't tell if he's afraid of me or of the vendors. Maybe it's both. My heart aches to think there are more like him, more starving children and families, living not far from the castle. The Brightcasters should be doing more for these people. They're part of our kingdom, aren't they? So why are they starving? Why aren't they a priority?

The boy reaches for the basket and his timid smile transforms into the brightest of grins. He scampers off, and when I turn to walk back to the castle gate, organizing my story in my mind once again, I stop short.

Standing all together, not five feet away, the four Brightcaster princes stare directly at me, each with varying expressions of disbelief on their handsome faces. My cheeks heat because I've been caught, but also because I refuse to apologize or make a fool of myself. Not to them. Not for helping a hungry child in *their* kingdom.

I fold my arms firmly over my chest. "What?" I raise an eyebrow. "Anyone have something they'd like to say?"

Dean scowls, his broad shoulders straightening against his leather vest. He's the oldest of the brothers and the most likely to become the next king, so I'm used to him overseeing things like they are his problem. Overseeing me like *I'm* his problem. Owen bursts out laughing so hard that his blonde hair bounces and his blue eyes water. Silas, Owen's twin, elbows him in the ribcage and scowls at me, just like his older brother. If it weren't for the light hair and eyes, he'd match Dean with his broody expressions. Bram is the youngest of the bunch. Since he's the only one who's not Dragon Blessed, he gets the least amount of attention. And I'll admit, from myself as well, even though we're the same age. His emerald eyes aren't locked on me like his brothers'. Rather, they stare intently at the vendors behind me, as if he's working through a math problem in that big brain of his.

"You gave that boy a lot of food," Bram states dryly. "I assume his family is in need."

"Because she's got a heart," Owen adds.

"Except now we don't know who that family is," Bram sighs. "The kid is gone."

"Where'd you get the money?" Dean asks, fiery eyes narrowing as he changes the subject.

"She probably stole it." Silas winks. "Not such a good little girl, are you?"

"That's none of your business," I snap. "Any of you." Even though stealing it was exactly what I did!

That sets Owen off laughing again. Truth is, Silas is right. I nicked the coins from Father's chest this morning, just in case there was an entrance fee to the tournament, or I had to pay somebody off. Turned out lucky for the boy, now didn't it?

"If you don't mind," I say casually, "I have to get back."

"You're coming with us," Dean states, his eyebrows furrowing together.

I laugh and start to walk away.

"It's okay," Bram says loudly. "We'll get you back into the castle without any problems."

I expect one of them to protest but nobody does. There's a bit of a crowd forming around us, so perhaps that's why. But the princes don't really seem like the type to care.

I turn back, opening and closing my mouth with surprise.

"I think you broke her," Owen laughs, his blue eyes shining.

I've grown up with these boys. But still, I wasn't expecting them to help me so easily. Especially not Dean. While the brothers and I have had times of childhood friendship and of teenage indifference, I've never known Dean to cover for me. He's usually such a stickler for the rules. And Bram, he's never cared about me at all. Silas just loves to stir the pot. Owen, too.

I shrug. "Fine." On the exterior, I try to be disinterested because inside, I'm thrilled.

This is perfect. No castle guard would dare question the princes about something like this. I don't have to sell my story about running for help because of the fire. All I have to do is walk alongside the princes and pretend I was with them all along. And so I do, and from the corner of my eye, I study them each in turn.

Do they know what I was really doing out here today?

Do they know anything about the fire I caused?

Do they suspect me?

I rub my sweaty palms along my dress and I start to hang back. Owen slows with me, leaning in close to whisper in my ear. "Nice job, by the way."

"About what?" I whisper back, my heart speeding.

He smirks, brushing his long blonde out of his eyes. They match the blue sky, even though he's not an air but a water elemental. Air is electric violet, but water is the kind of blue a girl can get lost in if she's not careful. "Nice job about the things you've done and the things you want to do. You're going to change this kingdom, you know that?"

My cheeks burn but my spirit lifts. "For the better?"

That sets him off again, his laugh catching the glares from his brothers. "Let's hope so."

5

THE SCENTS of garlic and melted butter, yeasty bread, and slow-roasted beef do very little to boost my appetite. I'm not hungry. I'm not even thirsty. All I am is nervous. Nervous, and excited. So I sit quietly in my chair, watching as those around me enjoy the food that is tasteless to me. And in my mind, all I can imagine is what it will feel like to fly again.

Once a week, all of Drakenon's court are invited to dine together. My family's status means that we're not only invited, but we're honored guests with the privilege of sitting right next to the royals at the head of the longest table. It's nothing new. We do this every week, afterall. Yet, tonight, I'm not myself. I don't carry on conversation, which I can normally fake even if I'm annoyed. And I don't eat. I don't even breathe as I should. The nerves are so strong that my palms sweat and my voice shakes and my heart thuds against my ribcage.

The tall stone walls echo the clattering of silverware and the low buzz of conversation that carries on around me. It's centered on one thing: the tournament. It's scheduled the day after next and I'm certain at any moment my secret plans to compete will be revealed. The charged energy of anticipation is practically tangible in the dining hall as everyone speculates on what is to come—myself included.

It's a high distinction to be enlisted to the dragon army. Many of the court are either part of the army already or have family who are, and because of that, everyone has a favorite for the tournament. People are already placing bets on the outcomes, already squabbling over the names written on the long list of entrants, as if each contestant wasn't a living, breathing, individual with just as many hopes and dreams as the rest of us.

I wonder if anyone is curious about the name nobody has heard of before: Raven Blaze.

"The competition isn't nearly what it used to be," Silas mocks, drinking a heavy gulp of wine from his chalice. He shakes his blonde hair back and rolls his stormy-sky eyes. "They'll let anyone into the dragon army these days, won't they?"

"Hardly seems like we're in a position to turn anyone away." Dean's tone is dry. "And what do you know of how things used to be? You're hardly old enough to remember anything different." At nineteen, Dean is only two years older than Silas, but he might remember the old ways. It only changed twelve years ago. That's not so long.

The glare is like a tightening rope between the two boys, neither refusing to let go.

"We've heard all the good stories." Owen leans forward, voice cheery, as he comes to Silas's defense. He always does that for his twin, no matter how insufferable Silas gets. "You know, of when the tournament wasn't merely a set of tests to prove skill, but actual battles between dragons, sometimes ending in death!"

"It was a bloodbath," Silas coos, as if that is something to be proud of.

Bram sighs, looking up from a tattered and probably well-loved book. "Most of those stories are gross exaggerations. It's better now that a dragon's only competition is him or herself. Let them prove they're good enough through a series of obstacles and let's be done with it. Nobody dies. Less waste of valuable resources."

"And what would you know of it? You're not even Dragon Blessed," Silas scoffs.

It's the unspoken rule around here: don't mention Bram's inadequacy.

Bram's shoulders tense and our side of the table goes quiet. I can feel my cheeks redden for Bram. If it were me, I'd respond by hurling an insult straight back at Silas, like maybe how he doesn't have any real friends because nobody wants to put up with his snotty attitude, or maybe how he's been drinking too much wine lately and starting to blend in with the more embarrassing members of the court. But I can't say those things, Mother would kill me.

And Bram? He says none of those things either. He's always full of surprises. Relaxed, as if nothing Silas says could possibly bother him, he raises his eyebrow and holds up his book. It's a text chronicling the history of the tournament. "If you took the time to study Eridas history as I have, you would know."

Eridas. Not just Drakenon, but the realm at large. And there's more than just our realm out there, there's another one—a non-magical one—that we know about but that we rarely talk about.

"And what else have you been studying?" Silas sneers, his body stiffening. "How to fit in with the mortals in the human realm, right? Because you'd do better to live there and everybody knows it."

I gasp. Like I said, nobody speaks of the other realm. It's not our business. It's nothing to do with us, we don't belong there. So this? This is a slap in Bram's face.

"Silas, don't," Owen says, his voice pleading.

Bram is the smartest of the four brothers, it's a fact that goes uncontested. But he is also the only one of the princes who wasn't born Dragon Blessed, so he doesn't have an ounce of elemental magic and no dragon is waiting within. His eyes are as emerald green and his hair as oak brown as any earth elemental I've ever met, but still, the magic skipped him as it often does our citizens. *But it rarely skips a royal, that's what is so hard about this!* Their blood is simply too powerful. It's why I'm here, afterall. We must make sure the next generation is even stronger than the last, even if the thought makes my stomach churn.

"That's enough," King Titus cuts in—his tone is as sharp as the knife in his hand. It quiets everyone in the hall. He sets down his silverware and glares at Silas. He and Queen Brysta were holding a conversation with my mother, but it appears he had an ear tuned toward his sons' discussion as well. "We do not speak to each other that way. Ever." He says softer. He eyes each of his children down the table, one by one, and they all stare back. They know not to argue with their father.

Silas's mouth forms into a thin line but he nods.

"You are *all* valuable and *all* needed," the King continues. "No matter who I choose to become the next king, you must all continue to train and prepare as if it is to be you. And you must all respect and love each other, or else things will get dangerous very quickly."

It's happened before. Brothers killing brothers for the throne. One look at Brysta's haunted eyes and I know it's her worst fear.

Titus raises his brows toward Bram. "Even you, son, must prepare. You will do whatever you can to learn and be ready, because even though it won't make you the king, it will prepare you to be his closest advisor. The Gods picked you to be in this family for a reason too."

As much as I loathe Titus sometimes, he loves his sons, each one, unconditionally. Of that, I am certain. I can hear it in his voice. See it in his eyes. And it's admirable. Respectable. His special brand of love. And it's also no wonder he doesn't want me to fight or train, or to be myself. He's saving me for one of them.

Bram swallows, his face paler than normal. "Yes, Father. I will honor my family."

Titus nods to Silas. "And you will not dishonor any Brightcaster, do I make myself clear?"

"Yes, Sir. I'm sorry, Father."

"It's not your father you should be apologizing to," Queen Brysta adds in her quiet way. She's beautiful, as always. Reserved. Perfect. Everything I'm supposed to become.

"Sorry, Bram."

"It's fine," Bram says, but the brothers don't even exchange a glance.

The tension has only grown thicker, the opposite of what was intended. But that is the way it is with these boys sometimes. That's the way it is with everyone living as part of our Dragon court. Royals have a way of bringing out the worst in people. Some-times the best, but usually, the worst.

Titus stands, and the room, with its long tables filled with jovial subjects, goes quiet again. Outside the arched windows, the sky is inky black. Inside the room, the candlelight flickers from the chandeliers, dancing off the stone walls and hanging tapestries—lit by a fire elemental, no doubt. Maybe it was Dean. Everything about this room is powerful and hard, just like the royal family who commands us.

"Thank you for dining with us tonight," Titus bellows for all to hear. "We look forward to the upcoming tournament and the bounty it will bring our people. As is the custom, anyone who passes all the tests will automatically be granted entrance into the dragon army." Murmurs of approval sweep through the room.

And that's exactly what I'm counting on.

"I have another announcement to make as well," he continues. His eyes flick to me and my entire body goes cold.

Everyone in the room turns to stare. My palms are immediately sweaty and my back goes stick-straight. The corset underneath my elegant blue gown cuts into my ribcage. Breathe, Khali. Just breathe! Has he found me out? Is this where he tells everyone I've foolishly tried to enter the tournament? *Please no…*

"Khali Elliot's parents, my wife and I, are excited

to announce that our darling princess has reached the age where she is ready to be courted by my sons."

Ohhhh—this is almost worse!

"Beginning tomorrow, she will alternate time between all four princes on a weekly basis, getting to know them better and building deeper friendships."

Friendship? Oh, is that all I'm here for? I want to roll my eyes. Instead, I smile.

More murmuring ensues, but this time it's Bram's name whispered. Why would I need to spend time with him when he'll never be King? That's what they want to know. But this is the custom for someone like me and someone like him. Even if it wasn't, the King wants Bram to be treated according to his station.

"This will continue for the next few years until she turns eighteen and I name which one of my sons is to be her future husband."

It's Dean's name that is whispered next. Everyone expects the oldest son to be crowned and for good reason. My stomach flips but not in a bad way. Sucking in a breath, I brave a glance at him. He's staring right back at me, his gorgeous eyes assessing me carefully as if I were a puzzle he can't figure out. They're no longer fiery, but coal black. His are the only eyes I know that change this way. It means he hasn't used his fire element recently, and while the fiery orange eyes make my heart pound, the black make me forget everything all together.

"Of course they're never to be left alone with

her," he continues. His gaze roves over the crowd, and I suspect he's looking for those who are his unspoken enemies, the families next in line who would love nothing more than to take his place. "We will honor the treaty set forth by our ancestors, as is the way and the will of the Gods."

He raises his chalice and everyone drinks.

I'm not to be left alone with the princes... Of course not. I never have been. Why would this be any different? If one of the sons were to kiss me before my wedding day, they'd be exiled without question. This is the number one caveat to me being here, a way to prevent biases or real relationships forming between myself and anyone who might become my husband, or more important, *might not*. I'm to remain the virginal bride for my people. Me, and my magic, are to be kept sacred and untouched.

No matter what I want.

No matter how I feel.

No matter what I choose—because really, I have no choice.

❧ 6 ❧

Silas and I walk side by side down the cobbled city streets. We're actually making easy conversation, but I can tell he's desperate for this whole "spending time alone but not alone" thing to seem natural. But that makes it even more uncomfortable for me because deep in my gut I know he doesn't want me for me, he wants me for the crown. Do all the brothers feel that way?

We're crowded on every side by our guards and all the random people hurrying in the same direction. This path is the only way down to the tournament grounds without flying, so it's packed. Since I'm not allowed to fly like all the others and it's also my date time with him, Silas offered to walk too. Faros follows close behind but she's no help. Every time I shoot her a "come save me" look, she just smiles happily and nods like I'm doing everything right and to embrace this new development. I love her, I do, but sometimes I feel like she doesn't get me. She doesn't understand. Maybe nobody does.

The tournament grounds are beyond the city wall, where there is ample room to host dragons and all the people who want to see them—which is to say, everyone. This tournament happens for a few days every spring and is the highlight for many, and probably the only time most people leave the confines of their little towns. All the Dragon Blessed aged fifteen and up may enter the tournament. And if they don't qualify, they may try again for a total of five years. Most wait until they're older and better trained to even attempt it, but still, there are many who enter the minute they're old enough to try. I think of the two young boys who signed up before me, knowing they're probably just as excited and nervous as I am.

Either way, pass or fail, it's an honor to even be tested.

Most people in our kingdom aren't Dragon Blessed. We all have dragon blood because we're all descended from dragons somewhere along the line, but that doesn't always translate into dragon shifters. Neither of my parents are shifters. Faros isn't. Many of the court and most of the citizens aren't either. And of those that are, even fewer are also elemental dragons. Elements are rare. Fire is the rarest of all, making Dean extra special.

Perhaps that is why everyone is staring at Silas and me, because he's an air elemental, which is second to fire, and I'm all four elements. Or maybe it's simply because he's a royal and I'm destined to be the next queen. Maybe even *his* queen.

When we arrive at the stone gate to leave the city, the crowds are much thicker. The streets have bottle-necked all the people down into a sea of excitement and noise. People are waving flags and singing songs, and I find myself having a little bit of fun too. And why shouldn't these people be excited? They may have friends or family competing. To be chosen for the dragon army is about the highest paying job any Drakenon soul could earn. It's an honor.

People part for us, and we make it through the gate without issues. I try to smile, to look pleased to see everybody, but really, I'm quite nervous. I'm used to eyes on me and being surrounded by people, but not like this. Not so *many* of them. And not when I know that soon I'll be competing as well.

Outside the gate, sleeping tents are erected along the wall for as far as I can see to accommodate the families who have traveled from all over the kingdom with their hopeful sons and daughters. Some of the market vendors have brought their booths out here as well, and the whole area smells of wonderful spiced meats and yeasty pastries. People gather around the booths, buying and eating, clinking tankards of ale and calling out to each other in tones of celebration.

I've never seen so much life, never really been allowed to be this close to it.

I love it.

Even now, a few of the hopefuls are in their dragon form, showing off for the incoming hordes of people. The dragons are always black and winged, with sharp teeth and claws. It's hard to distinguish one from the next. Elemental dragons have glowing colored eyes that correlate with their magic and females are typically smaller, but that's about it.

Silas shakes his head and scoffs.

"What is it?"

He's quiet for a moment, surveying the crowd and then my face, as if undecided whether or not he can trust me.

"Seriously, what is it?"

He sighs and narrows his stormy lavender eyes at me. "Okay, be honest, do you think we can afford to have female dragons in our army?"

An icky sense of betrayal washes over my body because from his tone alone, I know what he's going to say next.

"Afford it? Of course," I reply hastily. I have to squeeze my hands into fists to keep my face passive. More than anything, I want to punch that self-satisfied look right off his face. "Women can do anything men can do."

He looks like he wants to laugh, his lips curling at the corners and his eyes bewildered but superior. He doesn't laugh though. "Yes! But women can also do what men cannot do, right?" He raises an eyebrow. "If we're going to continue to be strong, strong enough to keep our kingdom protected and our enemies away, we need to keep breeding as many Dragon Blessed children as possible. If women are in the army, we risk that."

"Breeding?" I can't hold it in any longer. My anger seethes off me and I glare at him. Underneath my skin, electricity crackles to life. "Is that what you think of me then? Am I a womb and nothing more?"

He freezes, and slowly his face transforms into a teasing smile. "I'm just kidding, Khali." He laughs. "Relax!"

I don't believe him. He wasn't kidding. But he knows how upset he's made me so he's trying to placate me, to make me think I can trust him. He's proved himself to be so much like his father in how he thinks, but even his father allows women to join the army if they qualify and if it's what they want out of their lives.

If Silas is the one to be crowned, will he take that option away?

Probably.

"Come on." He wraps a possessive hand around my upper arm and tugs me after him. "We're late."

Sure enough, trumpets sound, signaling the start of the tournament.

We hurry to where rows and rows of wooden

stands have been erected all along one side of the vast field. I already checked the roster: the tournament is scheduled to last three days and I'm to compete for my spot on the last day. I'm extra glad for that because it gives me time to study the tournament course and make plans. I'll have to be careful not to be found out before I can finish; staying in dragon form and not using the telepathic link will be critical to my success. I'm still trying to figure out how I'll hide my unique eyes. I haven't quite figured that part out yet, but I will.

I must.

I have to make this work. I have to prove my worth.

I can still be queen and bear many Brightcaster children. But I should be allowed to fight for a place in the dragon army and be allowed to enlist, just as all other Dragon Blessed have been granted. The treaties say that anyone who passes the course may join. That will be me. I'll do it, and then King Titus will have to let me follow my destiny! There are treaties for a reason and the royals are strict to follow them because it keeps the people happy. Once they see me in action, the citizens of Drakenon will want me fighting their battles. They'll demand it!

This is the story I tell myself, over and over and over, even though, deep down, some part of me fears that no matter what I do, it won't make a difference.

Because all I can think about is what Silas said about females being saved for breeding and I know he's not the only one who feels that way.

A DRAGON MUST BE FAST. A dragon must be strong. A dragon must be able to take direction through the telepathic link. They can be taught how to fight, how to kill, and how to win, but only if they have these other skills already. So the tournament reflects that, by first timing how fast and how well each of the dragons can fly. Then they have to move massive boulders across the field, using their teeth or claws, the strength in their legs—whatever they can. Finally, using the telepathic link, they have to complete some kind of obstacle specific to them, like flying in intricate patterns or retrieving something hidden. If they're an elemental, the final test will usually have to do with the magic. For instance, a water elemental might be sent to the bottom of the nearby lake or a fire element will have to burn something and then put it out.

That very idea of the water makes me shiver,

though. Merpeople live in the waters of Drakenon, and while we have a deal with them to leave each other in peace, that didn't stop them from using me as a game piece when I was a young child. But that's an awful story for another day, and I push it back into the recesses of my mind, where I like to keep it tucked away and forgotten. Or at least, I try to…

Silas and I sit on the bench in the designated area for the rest of his family and some of the highest ranking members of court. We're surrounded by flapping flags and stoic guards, and beyond that, the rest of the excited crowd. King Titus and Queen Brysta perch at the back of the group, above the rest of us. Bram broods in the far corner, his nose stuck in a book, as usual. Dean is by his father, eyes glued to the field; and even though I snuck a couple of glances his way, he hasn't returned even one. And Owen lounges directly behind Silas, who spends more time turned back and talking to his twin brother than to me. They may look alike, but they seriously couldn't be more opposite. Owen is fun and relaxed, easy going and doesn't take anything seriously, to the point of being reckless. Silas is almost as uptight and opinionated as my mother, which says a lot.

For the third time in a row, a dragon fails the timed flight, and the crowd groans in unison. Unless it's more than their fifth time entering the tournament, they'll be back next year, but even still, we're all rooting for everyone to succeed. The stronger our army, the better. The announcer stalks up and down the grassy field, calling out to bolster the crowd.

"Why didn't we get to compete?" Owen groans. "I would have passed, no problem."

"You know why. Because Dragon Blessed *royals* are automatically admitted to the army, for one," Silas replies with exasperation. "And also, because our army experience won't be like the others."

"Right." Owen leans forward between us excitedly, his eyebrows shooting up into his shaggy blonde hair. "We'll be calling the shots, not taking orders."

"Something like that." Silas's lavender eyes gleam.

Gods, these boys are annoying!

I fold my arms over my chest, returning my focus to the field ahead and the next dragon in the tournament. She's just passed her time trial and is in the process of moving the boulders, but she's pretty small and it's not going well. The crowd grows insolent, screaming and chanting her name. My earth element rumbles beneath my fingertips. If I wanted, I could move that stone for her, make it look like she did it all on her own. But I don't. I can't cheat, not for myself or for anyone else.

Frustrated, she sits back on her hind legs and roars into the air, the sound louder than the crowd itself. Her bluish-lavender eyes glow bright with magic and a gust of wind sweeps through the field, powerful enough to move the rocks without her physically doing it.

"Should that even count?" Owen yells over the howling wind.

"I don't think so," Silas replies. "That's too easy."

"Yes, it counts," I call back. "It still displays her strength. It's *her* magic, afterall."

The boys don't comment further.

And sure enough, the girl has passed onto the next round, one in which she is also quick to find success. The crowd is ecstatic, cheers louder than ever, as the first entrance to the army is announced.

Trinity Wells.

A win for women everywhere!

She shifts into her human form and raises her hands high into the air. She did it.

I want that to be me.

The rest of the day continues much the same, but I'm so inspired by Trinity that I start to forget about my nerves. About one in four of the dragons passes the trials and is announced successful. Through it all, Silas and Owen keep me entertained with conversation, laying off the "no women in the army" talk after I shut Silas down about Trinity. Bram remains off to the side, reading his book, barely looking up to partake in the excitement. Dean next to his father and never once comes down to talk to me or his brothers. Courtiers, advisors, and friends come and go, including my own mother. I stay as focused on the field as I can, looking for any advantages I might be able to use the day after next.

My day.

When it begins to grow dark and the last of the participants has tried—and failed—we pack up and walk back. This time Bram joins us. Owen, Dean, Titus, Brysta, and the rest of the dragons shift to fly back to the castle. I'm momentarily stunned to see Brysta change into a dragon and fly overhead, then towards home. She never shifts, as far as I know. But then again, I guess I don't know everything.

I'm not the only one who's stunned, the crowd goes crazy for the stunt.

"What have you been reading all day, anyway?" Silas asks his brother as we climb the street up the hill toward Stonehearth Castle. He doesn't shift, which is curious because the boy is a total show-off, but I think it's because this is our "date" and he wants to stay by my side as long as possible.

Bram gives him a sidelong glance and then shrugs. "It's an agriculture book, specifically about farming methods."

"Why?" I squeal, equally intrigued and horrified. I can't imagine having that amazing tournament as my entertainment for the day and choosing to read a book about farming instead.

"Our father says if he can figure out a way to make food production more efficient, he'll allocate more funds to feed the poor." Silas says it as if it's the most boring thing he's ever heard and couldn't care less... but my jaw drops.

"Bram! Are you serious?" I step closer to him, a smile wide on my face. "Is there anything I can do to help?"

He steps back. "Umm, doubtful."

"Hey, I'm smart," I scoff. "And I care about this. I might be able to think of something."

"I have no doubt you're smart, Khali," Bram replies, but somehow I think he does doubt it.

I'm so sick of this attitude with these princes, that somehow my womanhood means that I'm not worth anything to them.

"I have all the same tutors as you and your brothers," I challenge. And okay, I don't always pay attention as well as I should. But still!

"Hey, don't worry about it." Silas slides his arm around my waist and I force myself not to push him away. "Bram will figure it out. He's got the big brain in the family for a reason right?" He winks at his brother. "The Gods put you here to be an *advisor*."

The dig is obvious, and even though Silas has been picking on his little brother for as long as I can remember, I still find myself surprised.

"That's right," I say, coming to Bram's defense. "It's a good thing *you* have him. We're all lucky to have Bram."

Bram's cheeks redden and he brushes his disheveled chestnut hair off his face. "Uh, thanks." He looks around, uncomfortable. "I'll, uh, see you later."

And then he's gone, disappearing into the crowd and back to hiding away from us like he's so used to doing.

"Why are you so hard on him?" I turn to Silas. "It's not like he's your competition."

Silas grins and squeezes me tighter against him. "I'm not worried about any competition, Princess. I'll be king one day. You'll see."

He's so confident—so sure of himself. And my whole body becomes cold. Somehow, I believe he might be right.

8

I STAND at the barred window of my chamber, gazing mindlessly as the morning sun lights up the landscape below. Taking one final steadying breath, I make for the door, leaving the hastily scrawled note for Faros to let her know I've already left with Owen and will see her later. I hope she believes it. I also hope she can forgive me later.

I slip out into the hallway, being extra quiet as not to wake my mother, and continue on soft steps until I've exited our family's chambers entirely. I'm dressed for the day in one of my usual gowns, this time in pink, with a cape for outdoors, and as far as anyone out here knows, I've already had breakfast and have things to do. I wave down a young maid and hand her a second note.

"Take this to Prince Owen," I instruct, my voice as direct as when my mother talks to the maids. She nods, wide-eyed, and scurries away. In the note, I've told Owen that I'm not feeling well and will need to skip today's time with him at the tournament. We've been friends for ages, and out of all the princes, he's the only one who really has ever felt like a true friend to me. But even still, there's an unspoken barrier between us, one that I can't risk crossing by telling him the truth.

These lies will catch up to me later, and I can only hope that Faros and Owen will cover for me if it comes out sooner than later. But right now, I've got to get down to the tournament grounds before everyone arrives. I've got to be ready to take my turn.

I hurry up to the roof of the castle, pulling the long hood of my black velvet cape over my dark curls and hide my face as I step out into the sun. Dragons flying into the castle get monitored, but flying out is easy. With so many coming and going from the castle these days, I plan to slip out with the crowd. So I wait in the shadows for what feels like ages, trying to ignore the cold morning air, until a group of five men and women stride out onto the roof. They're dressed in army fatigues, laughing amongst themselves like they don't have a care in the world. When they shift and take to the skies, I shift also, jumping into flight and following close behind.

Flight feels as amazing as it did the first time.

As easy as walking.

As meant to be as life itself.

I take a few minutes to soar around the skies, making long sweeping circles above the city. I'm not the only one either. More and more dragons are taking flight, most likely warming up for the day ahead. There's a special camaraderie between us. Through the telepathic link I can hear people chattering, giving tips, handing out compliments, and connecting in a way I've never done with *anyone* in my human form.

But I want to.

More than anything, I want to belong with them, to *this* group. I want to be accepted.

I don't say anything and stay away from the others; keep my head down and my unique eyes down even more. For now it's required that I distance myself and I'm okay with that if it means what I hope it's going to mean, that I'll be able to enter the tournament undetected. Maybe I can compete with my eyes down, too!

My mind wanders back to yesterday. Day two of the tournament had been similar to day one, except it was my time to spend with Dean, and he barely spoke two sentences to me. Not that I minded the silence all that much; I was ridiculously nervous to talk to him anyway. But for someone who everyone says is going to be the next king, he sure doesn't try very hard to impress me. I forced myself to ignore any hurt feelings I had about it and instead focused on the tournament. That, and I did my best to stay away from Silas, who stared at me from his bench like I was the shiny new toy his parents had ordered him to share with his brother. It is clear to me, and likely to the rest, that Prince Silas doesn't like to share.

I land some distance from the tournament grounds, near an outcropping of trees that's away from the people and away from the massive lake. Both things I want to distance myself from today. If I end up getting ordered to go into the water, I fear I'll let the nerves get the best of me and I'll fail my test. I haven't been in that water since I was a child. One day I'll be brave enough to do it again, but today is not that day.

I sit back on my hind legs and wait for my turn. I'm only the fourth dragon of the day. It's early enough in the roster that my lies might not find me in time to stop what I'm about to do.

Something rustles in the trees behind me and I turn, staring intently into the shadows. I'm reminded of the morning I snuck away to practice my elemental magic. Something had been watching me then, too. I still don't know exactly what I'd seen that day but with the emotion of getting caught by Dean, I'd forgotten all about it. But now a wave of awareness sweeps over my entire body. I draw out my claws and bare my teeth. Whatever it is, if it's dangerous, I'm prepared to take it down.

But what steps from the shadows isn't anything I expect.

Or, I should say, *who* steps from the shadows.

Owen.

He holds up his hands, a smile playing at his lips. "Khali, is that you? It totally is, I'd recognize your eyes anywhere."

And there it is, exactly why this plan is never going to work! Not knowing what else to do, I shift back into my human form and push him into the cover of trees.

"How did you find me?" I hiss.

"I've been out looking for you ever since I got your note," he says, his pretty blue eyes twinkling in the stream of sunlight. "I knew there was no way someone as passionate about this stuff as you would miss the final day of the tournament. And that got me thinking about the day my brothers and I found you out in the marketplace, the same day they'd listed the sign up sheet for this thing. That's when I knew you were planning to enter."

He's so much smarter than I ever gave him credit! Grrr…

"I don't know what you're talking about." The lie sounds exactly what it is.

"Don't worry about me," Owen says. "I just wish I'd thought of it first, honestly. Maybe I can sneak into the tournament next year. I've always wanted to show them what I can do here, you know. Prove myself."

My mouth twists. "Me too."

"Ha!" he laughs. "I knew it. How can I help?"

"Are you serious?" I think I'm in shock!

"Of course."

"Cover for me." My voice is pleading but I can't help it. My fate is in his hands.

"Already done." He shrugs, like none of this is a big deal. Like *being alone* with me isn't a huge deal. "But we need to do something about your eyes. They're a dead giveaway."

My heart sinks. "I don't know what I can do. I have two different colored eyes. That's just the way it is." I start to ramble. "One brown and one blue, though if you look closely the blue one is kind of greenish and the brown has some red in there…"

"They've always looked brown and blue to me," he says, looking closer.

"Sometimes they change a little." I shrug. "Something to do with the magic, I guess."

He thinks for a minute, twisting the toe of his boot into the soil and staring up at the sky. "Did you sign up with an element to let the committee know what to plan for you?"

I nod. "Earth. And I'll only stick to earth until I'm announced as passed. Once they let me in the army, they can't go back on their word, right? It's the custom."

His eyes flash to mine. "Wait, this is about joining the army?"

I step back. "So what if it is?"

"But you're going to be queen."

"So? Who says I can't be queen *and* a fearsome

warrior, huh? There's nothing in any of the treaties that says I can't."

He pauses, eyes searching my face, until his mouth transforms into a slow grin. "Can't argue with that logic."

I sigh with relief.

"I've got an idea," he says, voice rising with boyish excitement. "You just need two brown or two green eyes to pull this off and have them all believing you're an earth elemental and nothing more."

"Okay…" I don't know where he's going with this.

"So use your magic to change your eye color." He says it like it must be easy.

I laugh. "Seriously?"

"Yes, seriously. Just try it, okay?"

I let out a stilted breath, but I close my eyes and concentrate anyway, bringing the earth element into my awareness and pulling it up, up, and up. I feel the magic swirling under the bones of my cheeks, and imagine my eyes turning green. I hold that thought solid in my mind until the magic builds to bright green.

I pop my eyes open.

Owen claps. "By the Gods, look at you! It totally worked!"

I blink. "It worked?" I almost can't believe it.

"Yes, your eyes are glowing green right now. It's awesome! You remind me of what Bram would've looked like if the magic hadn't skipped him. Poor kid!

The color is almost the same, I swear, except yours are glowing a little and his are just wicked green."

An inkling of tiredness passes through my body and I realise holding this magic here isn't going to be as easy. But at least it worked. So I let that fill me up until I'm close to tears.

I jump forward and pull Owen in for a tight hug. "Thank you."

"No problem, Princess." He squeezes tight and then releases me. "Now, I better get going. The first dragon is up."

"I'm fourth," I say, hardly believing it's almost time!

He winks. "Nice! So I'll see you soon."

Nervous energy races through my veins. My time is almost here—better make it count.

9

THE AIR CARRIES MY WINGS, lifting me higher as I lengthen my body and zip over the field. In the distance, the crowd chants my fake name, "Raven Blaze," over and over. It doesn't faze me because I know soon enough they'll be calling my real one. That thought pushes me forward until I'm nothing but a streak of black in the endless blue sky.

A whistle blows to indicate I've passed the timed flight trial and everyone erupts in cheers. Elated, I flip into a long barrel roll, showing off before I land perfectly. Careful to make sure the earth energy is still active throughout my body, and hopefully keeping my eyes green, I peer out to the audience for the first time since starting my trial.

Hundreds, maybe even thousands, of excited spectators dance and scream and chant for me. They're crowded in on the benches along the length of the huge field. And they're all looking at me, squeezed in together, pointing and waving. I've never seen this many people in one place and my heart pounds wildly with a million different feelings. My dragon-self is thrilled but my princess-self is nervous. *This had better work.*

The royal family has the best view of anyone, located squarely in the center of the rows of tiered benches. The Queen and King seem to be preoccupied, paying me little attention as they chat with friends. That is probably for the best, but my stomach twists anyway. I want the king to see this. Dean is sitting with his brothers today and the four of them look as relaxed as ever. Owen sits between Silas and Bram, smiling at me so big that I can see the whites of his teeth from all the way across the field. Father is still traveling, but my mother is sitting near the Queen, watching me with a neutral expression. I hope whatever story Owen gave her, she believed it. Faros is nowhere to be found.

Next it's my turn to prove my strength by moving a pile of boulders from one side of the tournament grounds to the other. I'm not the least bit worried, this will be easy. I fly over to the rocks, noticing that the dragons helping with the tournament have replaced several regular rocks with gleaming black lava rocks nearly as tall as I am. The edges are sharp enough to cut me if I'm not careful. It's not fair, having these newer, harder to move rocks. Are they testing me even harder because of my speed? Doesn't matter. I refuse to let that stop me. I wait for the whistle, my plan solid in my mind.

The second my time starts, I get to work, tuning out the raging crowd and focusing only on the task at hand. My body is already flowing with earth magic and it takes little effort to release it. It connects with the soil and rocks around me, and suddenly I'm aware of all the earth beneath me, the massive density of it, the thicker places of rock, the thinner places of erosion. It's almost like it's an extension of my dragon-self, another limb, waiting for me to tell it what to do. A single action, maybe even a simple thought, and it will respond.

I close my eyes and imagine what I want, for the earth to move, to quake, only in this spot, only where these rocks are waiting, and carry them across the field. Similar to what Trinity Wells had done the first day of the tournament. If she can do it, then so can I.

It works.

I don't even have to touch the rocks. The magic does it for me with so much more force than I ever thought possible. The ground shakes and pulses, pushing the heavy lava rocks so hard that they catapult into the air and fly to the other side of the field. I gasp, momentarily awed by what I've just done. I nearly roar, but before I can utter a sound, the rocks find their destination, careening into the earth with such colossal impact they shatter into countless pieces. The crowd is stunned silent and then all at once, erupts in cheers. The whistle is blown and my second trial is announced a success.

Now for the third, the one I haven't been able to plan for. I paw at the ground restlessly, waiting for my final chance, pushing the nerves away.

A man walks toward me, the same one I've seen give instructions to other dragons. He's dressed in fine clothes and wears a fake smile; he seems nervous to be near me. Perhaps he doesn't think I can control my earth element well enough to be safe. Or maybe it's something else that's got him worried.

I quickly check to make sure the magic is strong enough to keep my eyes green and luckily it feels the same as it has all morning. I can only hope it is. It must be. If he knew who I was, there's no way he'd let me compete. He'd turn me into the king straight away.

As he nears, I notice the oddest expression on his face, like the blood has been drained right out of it. He looks around, eyes shifting. He can't be that afraid of me can he? He's been working with dragons all week! Something isn't right with him, I'm certain, but before I can question it further, he speaks.

"You're to make the forest," he points to the outcropping of trees where I spent my morning hiding out, "grow all the way through the field."

My body goes cold. Is that even possible? How is this fair? They're asking so much of me! The other dragons didn't have to do something so hard. I want to shift into my human form to argue but I know I can't; it would give me away.

"You have five minutes," he says, then turns on his heel and runs.

What?!

I have no time to think, to argue, to do anything. The whistle sounds and all I can do is take action. I fly toward the forest, figuring being among the trees will make this easier for me.

The crowd isn't informed of what my instructions are, they'll just have to wait and see. But of all my years watching the tournament, and my deep study the last two days, I've never known the third trial to be something so difficult. Maybe someone really does know it's me, and they're trying to make me fail? Actually, that answer makes perfect sense.

Well, I'll prove to them I'm worthy. It would take an incredible earth elemental to be able to grow a forest in such a short amount of time. If anyone can do it, it's me.

I land in a heap in the middle of the tallest of the trees, branches and leaves flying all around as I try to fit my dragon body among them. Before I can question it, I close my eyes and will the forest to expand. I pull on every single bit of my element, pushing it harder than ever before. The other three, fire, wind, and water, are longing to be let free as well. But it's earth I need now. It's the only thing that can make this happen for me.

Please, I beg silently. *Please, please, please.*

Just as I felt the rocks and soil before, I feel the trees now. They're alive—peaceful beings who don't want to be disturbed. But I send my magic in, around, and through them, willing them to multiply. Asking them. Begging them. *Please.*

And then it happens, one by one, the trees give in. Their roots spread, new saplings springing up from the ground. I keep my eyes closed tight—I don't have to physically see it to know it's happening. I push the magic on and on and on, and the growth continues. The new trees mature in superspeed, growing to match their parents, tall and strong.

The forest spreads. Deeper. Thicker. Widening, on and on.

Finally, when I fear I have nothing left, I pop my eyes open. I can't tell if I completed the task. I don't know how long it's been. My muscles ache with exhaustion, but I push through the branches anyway and take to the sky again, flying above the canopy and stare out to the forest.

I gasp, a little roar sounding from my throat.

There are trees *everywhere*. They've overtaken everything. There is no more tournament field. But worse than that, there are no more stands. The crowds of people are displaced, all lost in the thickest forest Drakenon has ever seen. It's so dense, it pushes right up against the city wall, breaking it down in several places.

No. No. No! I didn't mean to!

As I get nearer, I hear screaming. Not cheering… screaming. Crying. Fear!

I fly forward, trying to locate the source of all the screams so I can help. I push down the part of me that wants to cry, that wants to rage with anger. This wasn't how it was supposed to go. It wasn't supposed to end like this. Did I still pass the test? Will they announce me as a winner, despite my power getting away from me?

I hope nobody got hurt.

And I'm selfish for thinking only of myself right now. Look what I've done!

Something flashes between the trees below me. Something dark. I squint, trying to make sense of what I'm seeing.

A man in a burgundy robe races through the shadows, right toward where the stands used to be.

No, not just a man. I know what that color of robe means. But it can't be. They can't travel through our borders because the wards are too powerful. Right?

But it is. It's an Occultist.

This is a warlock who belongs to the cult that is our greatest enemy—believing our elemental magic is blasphemy. They've ravaged their way through every kingdom in Eridas except for Drakenon. And one is right here; I have no doubt he wants us dead.

Has he been here all along? Was he the one watching me in the forest all those weeks ago? Has he been waiting for an opportunity to get to the royals? Maybe he put a spell on that man to give me the crazy trial, to create a diversion so he can attack. There's so many possibilities, and desperate to prove myself, I fed right into his plan.

Panic prickles over my entire body, but so does determination. I swoop toward him, claws and teeth bared, magic swirling within, ready to strike him down.

❧ 10 ❧

THE FOREST IS SO different from above than it is below. Down here, the foliage is thick and intimidating. And the people? *My* people? They run in all directions, screaming and frantic… because of me.

At first I don't understand why they're so afraid, and then I see it. A black smoke-like substance intertwines with the trees, long thin strings, wrapping around the branches and weaving through every hidden crevice. It snakes through the forest like it has a mind of its own. And as I wonder what it's for, it strikes, holding on to an innocent and forcing her to her knees. I shift back to my human form and leap, trying to fight it off, but how does one fight off smoke?

All around me, people writhe in pain, screaming incoherently, eyes fixed in far-off, glassy stares. Whatever it is, it's got a hold of their minds somehow. The harm is unbearable to watch. Someone cries, a child. I jump up and run to a nearby woman with her little girl, both caught in the tangles of the black smoke, and try to shake them out of it before it takes hold.

I'm too late.

It's as if they don't even know I'm there. The smoke has to be the work of this Occultist. And it's my fault. I played right into his plans and allowed him to attack our people, to put them in a vulnerable position where they couldn't get away from his magic in time.

Something grabs onto me, and I scream, falling to the rocky dirt. The black magic is curling its way up my leg and I'm powerless to stop it. My thoughts numb and a terrible sadness plummets over my entire body, from the inside out. I try to scream again, but nothing comes out. The black continues to climb up my body, pulling me deeper and deeper into anguish. I'm going to die. Somehow, I know it, deep to the very core of my being. It's sucking the life out of me. *This is it.*

No, I won't let this be the end. It can't be. I have to fight. I think of all I have left to do, of all the people counting on me to fix this. If not for me, I'll fight for them. I dig deep within me, underneath all that pain and sadness, until I find the spark of something urging to get out: my fire element. I hiss and extend my fingers, forcing the fire to fly from my fingertips. The second it touches the smoke, the magic snaps away, retreating. I'm left even more exhausted than before but I can't give up.

I stand, brushing myself off and looking around. I have to be careful; I don't want to set this forest on fire while so many innocent souls are lost within its hidden places. But if fire is what's going to release my people from this horrible madness, then fire is what I'll use.

Going to the mother and child first, I blast a small fireball as near to them as I dare, making sure to hit the smoke but not them. Like it did for me, the black magic releases the pair and slithers away to find a new victim.

They blink up at me, confused and dazed. "Go," I yell, helping them up. "Get out of this forest. Take anyone you can with you. Get as far away from the smoke as you can."

I don't know if it will matter. The Occultist is already here, isn't he? Maybe he's left his smoke to do the damage in the forest and he's already in the city.

Maybe he's not alone.

My heart races and I take off running, searching for the royal family, and releasing anyone I find trapped in the smoke along the way. If I were an Occultist here, I'd want to take down civilians in my way, but it would be the royals that I'd be after. They're the heart of the kingdom, afterall. And that strategy aligns perfectly with what everyone's been saying the cult has done in other kingdoms.

I follow the smoke, hoping it will lead me to something useful. Sure enough, it does. Part of the city wall has crumbled, succumbing to the trees. The smoke is thicker here. I hear the familiar voice of King Titus yelling orders from beyond the wall. I've never been so relieved to hear him! His army is probably preparing for the attack while simultaneously getting him and his family to safety. But what had Owen said? That they were trained to fight. They were part of the army, too. What does that mean, really?

I hold a fireball in my palm and race over twisted vines and under low hanging branches, trying to get closer to the action. I need to warn them about what they're up against. Or do they already know? As I push through to the other side of the city wall, where the stone streets are torn from the new growth of my forest, I see them. All of them.

Queen Brysta stands with Bram, King Titus beside them. Silas and Owen are both in their dragon forms, but I'd recognize those elemental eyes anywhere. Dean hasn't shifted to his dragon, not yet. But he holds fire in his palms, same as me. He stands in the front of the group, keeping the smoke at bay while his father yells orders to his generals.

I stumble forward. "There's an Occultist here," I yell. "I saw him. I saw his robes."

They all turn on me, eyes ranging from shocked, to relief, to murderous.

"Was that you?" King Titus hollers, eyes fixed

with rage as he looks me over. "Did you enter the tournament?"

Umm… shouldn't he be happy to see me safe and alive? How did he know it was me who entered the tournament? I gulp, my cheeks flaming. I don't say a word but I don't have to, it's obvious now. I can feel it on my face—the truth and my lies.

"What were you thinking?" Dean booms. "And you let an Occultist manipulate you? How did that happen?"

"Are you working with him?" Titus questions, his face red with anger. "Is that it?"

"No," I gasp, shocked he could even think such a thing. "I don't know how he got into Drakenon but I think he must have been waiting for the perfect opportunity to strike."

"An elemental must have brought him through the wards, right?" Dean turns to his father. "There's no other way through."

"No other way that you know of, anyway," I scoff.

"Khali, you made the trees do that?" Queen Brysta questions, her mouth turning down.

"Why? Why would you do something so reckless?"

"Because that was the task!" I scream, tired of defending myself. "Because nobody will let me train and nobody cares about what I want and so I entered the tournament. And growing the forest was what your man told me to do."

"Not for the tournament," Titus growls. "We'd never."

"Well that's what happened! Someone must have gotten to him. The Occultist, if I had to guess. It wasn't my fault!"

"Way to take accountability." Dean glares at me. "Really mature, Khali."

My chest burns with shame. But why should I feel shame? Why should I always have to defend myself over and over again? "We don't have time for this! We have to fight off this Occultist before he hurts anyone else."

Too late.

The black smoke-like magic appears out of nowhere and swarms all of us, thicker than before. Dean screams angrily and throws flames into the air and I do the same, but it's not enough. Not even close. And while Dean and I may be immune to burns, the rest of the group is not. We can't very well burn them up in order to fight off the magic.

It's everywhere, turning the sky to darkness, holding us in a blackness so vast, nothing is visible. The sadness returns, crushing me down until I fall to my knees and burst into tears. It's all my fault. I've failed my people, everyone, myself included. At first I can't believe this is really it, really the end, but then I start to accept it. My entire body grows tired, heavy with the truth that I'm about to die.

Suddenly, the darkness and all the smoke clears

away. But I'm immobilized and the magic might as well still be around us. Paralyzed by terrible sadness, but also like I'm underwater or buried alive or lost in an endless dream. I can't move my limbs. I can hardly think.

Everything is ruined. Everything is hopeless.

A creepy man in a dark red robe steps from behind the crumbled wall—the Sovereign Occultist. His scalp is shaved clean and his eyes glow red. His skin is smooth, the color hard to describe; almost like his cheeks are pale but the rest of him is dark. And he's ageless. I have no idea how old or how young he is. There's something about his magic that is making it extremely hard to pin down any visible discerning features. I've heard this is how they all are. Their magic camouflages them to look similar but seeing it now, seeing this strange ageless man, sends curling fear up and around my heart that squeezes tight.

He cackles and speaks but his voice is far away. I can't hear him, not really. I'm too caught up in everything I'm feeling and the anguish of the black magic. Desperate to fight it, I peer around. Everyone is in the same pain as myself. All the dragons have shifted back to their human forms, lying immobilized, barely seeming to notice the Occultist at all.

He pulls a dagger from his robes.

Steps towards Dean.

No!

Everything in me sparks to life, every magic

bursting forth. I jump up, screaming, and shift into my dragon self in a matter of seconds. And then I open my mouth and release all the fire within me onto the Occultist. And on to Dean.

I don't let up. Dean will be okay.

The Occultist won't be so lucky.

He screams, burning alive. He shoots his black magic at me again but I don't let up. After what feels like forever, Dean snaps out of whatever hold is on him and joins me, doing the same but with fireballs flying out of his hands.

I grow weak, falling to my knees, then shift back to my human self.

"I've got this," Dean yells. And not only does he take charge, but other dragons from the army appear to help. The Occultist is fighting back with his magic, trying to protect himself, but it's impossible, he can't hold out forever.

Dean must get tired, because he stumbles back as I did. The other dragons take over the job.

The Occultist was on his knees but now he's on his back. And then quick as a blink, he's gone, burned into nothing but a pile of ash. The black smoke fades into nothing, his magic gone with him. My eyes flutter closed and I fade right along with it.

❧ 11 ❧

I WAKE up to my body jostling up and down. Wind blows against me, loud in my ears. My eyes are heavy as lead. My limbs pulse with pain and my breath is long and slow. Forcing consciousness, my eyes flutter open and I gaze from side to side. The sky is brilliant red, the time just as the sunset glows brightest. It takes a moment for me to realize what's happening, but when I do, I gasp.

I'm being carried on the back of a dragon, an experience I never expected I'd have. It startles me and I lift my head up, gripping on tight at the same time. It's incredibly rare for a dragon to carry anyone on their back because it's seen as a dishonor to both the human and the dragon. But here I am, flying through the sky, a league of six other dragons surrounding me on all sides.

It all comes rushing back, the memory of what

happened. The tournament. My task. The Occultist and everything that happened. I'm certain he's dead, which is the only thing that gives me a small bit of reprieve. There's nowhere for me to go. My magic is there underneath my skin but it's way too weak to access right now. And my dragon is waiting but she's tired. And what would shifting do for me? I'm surrounded by King Titus's army—I have to be. He's ordered for me to be taken somewhere, but where? There's a mess to clean up back at Stoneshearth and I want to be there to help. Not here. Not this!

After what feels like forever, after the sun sets and night turns to blackness and the air grows cold, we finally land. The moon hangs bright and full in the sky. Stars spread out above us like an eternal blanket. It's enough to light up the landscape and it's beautiful but I can't admire it.

We're still somewhere in Drakenon, I'm sure. Things look much the same, mountainous and forested, rocky and beautiful. But judging by the bitter cold, I'm guessing we flew north of the castle. Again, I want to know why. Am I being punished for what I did? What does that mean?

Thankfully, the landing was smooth. I scramble off the dragon as soon as I'm able. He shifts, turning into a man I recognize as one of the king's most trusted guards. The rest of the dragons shift too. All three of the Dragon Blessed brothers are here— Dean, Silas, and Owen. The princes don't look at me.

The king, he's here too, with another of his guards, and *he* looks at me like the insolent child he believes I am. His guards do the same.

"What's going on?" I demand, my voice hoarse from my screaming earlier followed by the recent disuse. "Why are we here?"

"I can't have what happened today derail my family's future," King Titus says, and that's all before he turns and walks away. The group follows and one of his men pushes me along after them. A sinking feeling settles into my stomach. I don't like this.

The pine forest ahead is thick, and when I squint, I can just make out the flicker of light between the trees. A fire, perhaps? We shuffle down an overgrown path in a single file line. I finally make out where the light is coming from. Ahead, tucked between the trees, is a small cottage. It's constructed from logs and stone, barely anything more than a hovel. Who could possibly live here that we would be visiting in the middle of the night? Whoever it is, it can't be good.

King Titus knocks on the door and it swings open to reveal an old wizened looking man. He peers at us from round spectacles. His skin is pale and his beard and hair are white as snow. His eyes are deep brown and match the simple cloak he's dressed in. Nothing about his appearance is overtly abundant or special, but his energy, it's overflowing with magic. Not elemental magic. Not the magic I felt on the

Occultist. This is different, it's most definitely special —and a little scary.

"Ah," he says, "I wasn't expecting you, Your Majesty."

"I know," Titus replies in a careful tone, "I'm sorry to drop in like this but it's an emergency. May we enter?"

The man looks over our group and then holds the door open. "Of course." He motions for us to enter, and I think there's no way all eight of us will fit in his tiny home, but when we step inside, it expands to two stories high and as wide as the banquet room back home. Magic at its finest. The place is filled top to bottom with wooden bookcases and drawers, all of which slam shut before I can get a good look, hiding the contents inside from our curious gazes.

"This is Aleeryrick," Titus says, eyes narrowing on his sons. "He's a long time friend of the Brightcaster family."

"What is he?" Silas asks, raising his blond brow, mischief sparking behind his lavender eyes.

Aleeryrick takes a deep breath. "I'm a sorcerer."

The room falls silent. No one like him is allowed in Drakenon. The merfolk have struck a deal with us to stay here, but besides them, there are no witches, wizards, fae, sorcerers... there's nobody but us elemental dragon shifters. It's been that way for at least a century when the Brightcaster family took possession of the throne and secured the borders.

His being here is a crime, isn't it? And the king *allowing* him to be here—that's treason, is it not?

"Aleeryrick is an immortal," Titus says, "and he's the reason the wards are as strong as they are. He's the reason the treaties can't be broken—he fortified them for us. And it's his magic that has allowed our kingdom to thrive."

I frown. It's the first I've heard of anything like this. From the confused expressions on the princes' faces, they must be thinking the same.

"And what's in it for him?" Dean asks, eyeing the sorcerer skeptically.

Aleeryrick laughs. "Privacy. Safety. Wealth. Take your pick."

The sorcerer turns to Titus and smiles. "And you've brought the newest princess. Why?"

Titus looks at me for a long moment. I'm frozen in place, unsure of what to do, what to say, or how to feel. "Khali is dangerous. She knows too much of her own strength."

What?

Foreboding washes down my body. I don't like where this is going.

"I need you to change her memories." Titus sighs. "She must forget having ever competed in the tournament."

My mouth hangs open and I'm stunned. Aleeryrick nods, like it's nothing to him. Any good feelings I had toward him vanish instantly.

"No!" I hiss. "Don't you dare touch me."

The two guards move in and detain me, holding me tight in their meaty fists. I pull at my elemental magic, determined to break free, but something presses back, holding it down. Something different. Something new. Aleeryrick.

I shake my head and plead with anyone who will listen. "Don't do this. Please! I'll get in line, I promise. Don't hurt my mind. Don't take my memories. Please!"

"Are you sure about this?" Owen asks, his voice shaking. "I think she already learned her lesson."

"Father, reconsider," Dean adds. "This is too extreme."

Silas stays silent.

I wish Bram were here, he'd be able to talk sense into his father. No, I wish *my* father were here. He would never stand for this!

"It has to be extreme," Titus snaps. "What happened has upset the balance I've worked so tirelessly to maintain." He turns back to Aleeryrick. "Not only that, the memory of what happened today also needs to be changed for all the minds of Drakenon that are not standing here with us in this room today. There needs to be no memory of the Occultist who broke into our lands and made an attack on my family. The fear is already upsetting the balance of power, we can't have that." He levels his eyes on the sorcerer. "Can you do that?"

Aleeryrick is still for a very long time but then he smiles slowly. Some of his teeth are rotten. "That will take some intricate spellwork."

"Name your price."

The sorcerer raises a bushy eyebrow, excitement sparking his expression. He turns on me. "I want her oldest child to be my apprentice."

"You can't make a deal on my behalf!" I snap. "No way!" A hand clamps over my mouth.

Titus is quiet for a long moment before speaking. "Only if she has a daughter." The brothers exchange worried glances. Someone like me rarely has daughters, but what if…

"Any daughter? Even if it's not her oldest?" Aleeryrick clarifies.

"Yes."

"Deal."

No!

But it's done. A long onyx staff appears in the sorcerer's right hand. He grips it tightly between gnarled fingers and slams the end into the floor— once, twice, three times. The room lights up with the brightest white I've ever seen. I close my eyes against it, blinded. And then the rest is forgotten.

❦ 12 ❦

THE ORCHESTRA MUSIC envelops the room, the sweet melody of strings adding elegance to the ball. The banquet hall has been cleared of tables and instead is lit with glowing candelabras that hang like golden ornaments from the ceiling. All the members of the court are in attendance, dressed in their finest. The women wear corseted gowns and the men in elaborate coats of rich coloring. People stand in groups, chatting idly, happy smiles on their rosy faces. Couples dance, twirling about the room, dress skirts flying behind them in a rainbow of silks.

I should be happy. Why aren't I happy?

I normally enjoy these events more than the overdone dinners, with too much wine and too much talking. In these situations, I can dance if I'm in the mood or I can hide out in a shadowy corner until it's appropriate for me to leave early. But there's something not right about tonight, a ball of energy in my chest that I can't quite place. Something is missing and I can't figure out what it is. It's driving me crazy!

The tournament ended three days ago with little fanfare. Mostly everything has returned to normal. The travelers have packed up and gone home. The wall has been mended, though I can't quite remember exactly what happened to it in the first place. Every time I try to think of it, my mind wanders away. Anyway, tonight we get to honor those fortunate souls that have proved worthy enough to be admitted into the Dragon Blessed army. I'm happy for them! I wish it could be me. Maybe one day. It would be so exciting, but that's a wish for another time…

The new recruits have been invited to join the rest of us for the ball, and now I recognize many of them simply because they're surrounded by adoring fans. The girl from the first day catches my eye and I smile. She was the first dragon who qualified. My chest aches when I look at her, with happiness, but also with envy for myself. Oh how I wish I was Trinity Wells. But then the thought of myself being in the army slips away too.

"Can I have this dance?" a male voice asks.

I turn to find Owen smiling down at me. I can't refuse any of the princes a dance, can I? But I guess, of them all, Owen is my favorite. Of course Dean makes my heart race. But Owen is the one who makes me feel at ease. And that is almost better. Almost.

I nod, and he sweeps me into his arms, spinning into a waltz we both know well. For years, part of our studies here include dancing so this is almost as natural as walking.

"Are you okay?" he asks, his bright blue eyes narrowing in concern.

It's unexpected, that look on his face.

I don't know if I've ever seen him look at me that way. He's usually silly, never serious. "Of course," I answer. "Why do you ask?"

He gazes around, straightening his spine, and pulls me a little bit closer. "You really don't remember, do you?" His voice is quiet. Upset. Angry.

Something tugs at that ball of strange energy I've been carrying but it doesn't let loose.

"I don't know what you're talking about." I frown. Or do I? Hmm…

He pauses for a second, looking me up and down. Then he finally nods, but his face is sad and I want to know why.

"What's going on, Owen? What aren't you telling me?"

He lets out a long breath, like he wants to tell me, like he's so close, but something is preventing him. "What do you think of all this?" he asks instead.

"All what?" I pout.

He gazes around the room. "The people who made it into the dragon army. How does that make you feel?"

I bite my lip but honesty comes out of my mouth, even if I know better. "I'm jealous. It should be me."

He nods once. "I agree."

It's the second time he takes me by surprise tonight.

I stare into his eyes, waiting for him to make a joke, but he never does.

"So what are you going to do about it?" he asks.

The music and surrounding chatter is loud enough that I'm fairly certain nobody can overhear our conversation, but still, his question makes me nervous. Can I trust him?

Deep down, I know I can.

"I want to train," I admit. "But I can't. Your father won't allow me."

"What if he doesn't know about it? Would you train then?"

I stare at him, looking for a crack, a tell, something… but he's being honest. He means exactly what he says.

"Are you saying you're going to help me?"

He nods once. Only once. But it's enough.

My heart jumps. I believe him. And for the first time all night, my smile is actually genuine. I'm so excited!

"May I cut in?" Dean's low timbre makes my heart skid and I don't know that I can handle any more, but here I am, smiling even wider.

Owen winks at me. "Of course, big brother. She's all yours."

And then he's gone. Dean is in his place, and I can hardly breathe.

"Hey, you." He smiles, dark eyes sparkling as he gazes down at me. "Are you having fun?"

I am now! I can hardly speak, but at least I can nod. I can't help it: I smile and smile and smile. My crush must be obvious but I don't even care. Dean has never asked me to dance before.

"You look beautiful tonight," he says, eyes flicking down to my silver dress. It fits me like a glove and accentuates all the right curves, making me feel older than I am. When Faros dressed me in it earlier, I imagined Dean admiring it, but never did I think that would actually happen. I almost can't believe it!

"Thank you," my voice croaks. "So do you."

The next hour goes by in a blur of heavy glances and easy conversation and lots of dancing. I can hardly believe it; this is nothing like the Dean I've grown up with. He's always kept away from me, never letting me in, barely even speaking to me. And now I have to believe he's romantically interested in me? Is it only because he's vying for the throne?

I don't know what to think. Not that it's easy to think when I'm around him. It's hard, what with my heart pounding and his amazing woodsy scent filling my nostrils and the warmth from his body pressed against my own. I want to crawl up right into his chest and get lost in his arms. I want so many things I shouldn't want.

I can't.

I can't even kiss him. I can't kiss anybody until the king announces who my fiancé is, and that won't happen for a little over two years. Not until I'm eighteen.

This is harmless flirting. That's all it can be.

"Come on," he whispers, his lips too close to my ear. A shiver runs down my spine.

"There's something I want to show you."

He wraps his fingers with mine and no less than a few people around us watch as he tugs me from the room. In the distance I catch Silas glaring. Titus and Brysta have noticed. Bram is there too, watching with a perplexed expression.

"We shouldn't be alone," I whisper as we stumble out into the hallway.

"Don't worry," he says. "I won't tell if you don't."

Those words are loaded with so many things.

And before I can form a coherent response, we're speeding up one of the staircases that leads to the roof and I don't protest because even though I know what I should do, I also know what I want to do, and that wanting part is winning.

We step outside and breathe in the cool spring air. The moon is waning but still bright, light enough to illuminate the cloudy sky. The clouds are so thick that I can't see any stars. Something about the thought of stars prickles at my mind. When was the last time I looked at them? I can't remember, and it bothers me for some reason, like I should be able to remember, like it's important that I do.

Dean pulls me into his arms, his heated hands running up and down the goosebumps that have crept along my arms.

"Hey," he says, smiling in a way that makes my insides all melty. "Do you trust me?"

I nod and lick my lips. His eyes flash to the movement. And then his lips are on mine. It's so unexpected, so sudden, that I freeze. He can't do this. We can't do this. But I breathe him in and sigh, and between breaths our lips meld together in perfect harmony. All worry disappears and I tug him in closer, deepening the kiss. I'm flooded with memories of what it was to be up here all those weeks ago, when I took the leap and flew. The thrill of it had been made even better by the fact that it was forbidden. The feeling it was right was what urged me to take that jump, even though everyone wanted me to believe it was wrong.

They were wrong.

And this? This kiss? It too, is so, so right.

"Princess," a voice gasps. "Is that you?"

Dean and I rip away from each other. My cheeks heat. His face pales. But there's something else in his face too—resignation?

"Prince Dean," another voice adds, shocked.

The two guards stare at us like they can't believe what they're seeing. But they've seen it. We've been caught. And none of us can undo it.

"Come with us," one says to Dean. "We have to take you to your father and announce what you've done."

"But the king is with the entire court," I plead, desperate. "Shouldn't this be handled in private?"

"It can't," the other says, his tone is pained, like he wishes he didn't have to follow orders. Not even the Brightcasters are immune to the treaties. The rules must be followed. I'm not exactly sure how, but some kind of magic forces us to comply.

Dean looks back at me and gives me a small smile and a nod. "It's okay, Khali. It's all going to be okay."

"It was my fault," I lie, pleading with the guards. "I kissed him. He wasn't kissing me back."

The guards stop, studying me skeptically. But they want to believe me, don't they? They're loyal to the Brightcasters. If I convince them that this was all me and not Dean, maybe I can get them to let it go.

"Don't," Dean says, staring down at the ground. He won't meet my eyes. "This wasn't Khali's fault. I kissed her first."

"No," I cry out, but it's too late. They haul him between them and tug him toward the exit.

"I'm so sorry." My voice is hollow. I shouldn't have kissed him back.

Dean shakes his head but he still doesn't look at

me. "This isn't your fault, Khali. Trust me on this. Please."

And then he's being carried away. I follow, but I know there's nothing I can do. I've heard the stories. We all have. I know the rules. We all do. Dean is going to be sent into exile. He'll never be crowned king now. He'll be forced to live a life away from his family.

And it's all because of me.

Even if he says it's not, I know it is. Any other girl. He could have kissed any other girl in the entire kingdom and this wouldn't have happened! But he chose me and there's nothing we can do. What's done is done.

As I follow them, hot tears streak down my cheeks. Tears of embarrassment. Regret. But mostly of pain, for I know that not only will I mourn his loss, but his brothers, his parents, his friends, the entire kingdom, everyone will be heartbroken.

Where will he go? What will he do? Will he survive outside of Drakenon? What will happen to his magic? What will happen to our kingdom? To me?

These are the questions I shouldn't have to be asking right now. And then there's the one that slams to the forefront of my mind.

Did Dean do this on purpose?

Because wait…

His sudden interest in me was so out of character, as was his blatant disregard for the treaties. He knows the rules just as well as anyone. He's always been one to follow the rules. The idea that he did this on purpose is the only explanation I can possibly think of, and suddenly the blood hot in my cheeks is there for another reason—another question.

Did Dean use me in order to leave Drakenon?

It's too late to ask and his face is still resigned, as if this was his plan all along. My heart beats are frantic and my thoughts are frenzied because I can't stop this and I can't change this. When we enter the banquet hall, our crime is announced. We're met with shock, with outrage, and questions—so many questions—but one thing is undeniable, Dean has to leave. My heart shatters into a million pieces, for losing him, for being used, for everything I'll never get to choose and for all the things that will be chosen for me.

THE END...
    FOR NOW

WHAT'S NEXT?

THANK YOU FOR READING! If you enjoyed this book, please consider leaving a review. Don't forget to read the Dragon Blessed trilogy, part of the Bleeding Realms world, available in ebook and paperback, with audio coming soon.

Bleeding Realms: Dragon Blessed
    Crown of Dragons Book One
    Kingdom of Spirits Book Two
    Throne of Embers Book Three
    Turn the page for an excerpt of book one!

CROWN OF DRAGONS EXCERPT

Chapter One - Hazel

A woman with a butcher knife sticking out of her back is pulling my hair. At least, she's trying to. She hasn't quite figured out that I can't actually feel her, so she's gone from the polite ask, to the shoulder tap, to full-on hair pulling.

It's a new low, even for me.

I shift away, biting back an annoyed growl, and attempt to focus on the classroom whiteboard where Dr. Peters is scrawling something about Aristotle. I blink, hoping to tune out this obnoxious lady who's now flashing images of her medicine cabinet at me like she's going to die if I don't help, and I'm seriously about ready to punch her in her dead, pasty face.

Not that it's even possible. But seriously!

"You okay?" Macy whispers from the seat next to mine.

I sink into the padded chair and refocus on the lecture hall as I nod, hoping she'll forgive whatever horrible nonverbals are morphing my expression at the moment. Macy is kind and cool and pretty, and dang it if I don't want her to be my friend.

Yup. I've turned into *that girl*.

It's only been a week since I started my freshman year of college, and I've already managed to join what's turning out to be our dorm's "in crowd." Don't ask me for tips. Considering that I graduated a year early from high school over what Mom so lovingly calls "The Regina George Situation", I don't have any tips.

I moved into my dorm last Sunday, only one day before classes started, because I didn't want to be noticed. I didn't have visions of grandeur, of being tossed a frisbee my first day by my future husband or something equally moronic. Quite the opposite. I was awkwardly trying to blend in with my oversized hoodie from the sales rack at Target, my dirty blonde hair pulled back into a ponytail, wearing the barest of makeup (no contouring here), and hiding behind my nerdy and totally fake black-rimmed glasses. Which, by the way, I love—I'm proud to call myself a nerd.

I shouldn't have stood out, and I definitely shouldn't have made friends effortlessly. But did that stop the other girls living in my dorm from sticking to me like white on rice? No. No, it did not. And so far the "Mean Girls" group in our dorm is turning out to be the opposite of mean. They're like the glittery unicorn group of girly friends I'd always dreamed of having but only thought existed in cheesy made-for-TV movies. Who even knew pretty and popular *and* *kind* was possible at our age? But Mom promised college would be different, and so far, she wasn't lying.

The dead lady is still hovering right in my eyeline, distracting me from whatever's going on up front with Doctor Peters. It's pretty clear that she was a drug addict and she's going through some major withdrawals. I don't quite understand how that works considering she no longer has a body, and I feel bad for her—I do. But I'm *also* trying to focus on Peters as he goes over the origins of anthropology, and she's making herself rather difficult to ignore. I catch my other new friend Cora's raised eyebrows from across the room, and she points to her phone before turning back to the lecture. Discreetly, I check mine to find her text.

Wanna study for Friday's quiz together at lunch? My treat ;)

I smirk. The dining hall is included in our dorm fees, so it's not like Cora's going to treat me to anything other than the pleasure of her company. I quickly text her back. **Sure. So generous of you ;)**

I'm lucky this class has my two newest besties in it. Okay, they are the only true friends I've made so far, but still, it's best friend status at this point with the three of us. We've spent nearly all our time together over the last few days since we met. I wish all my classes had them, but no, that's not how college works. We just caught a break with Anthropology. Yay for General Education, or something like that.

Cora waggles her eyebrows with a cheeky grin when she reads my reply, and I'm hit with this surreal feeling of imposter syndrome. I'm suddenly cool, aren't I? How is that possible? It won't last and I hate that I care. This stint at popularity is a total farce that hasn't done a thing to change how I feel inside. I still feel out of place. I still have anxiety every single second I'm around these "normals" because deep down I know these people won't understand me and will probably mock me once they figure out my secret. Because they *will* figure it out. Given time, everyone does. Try as I might, I can't help my freak flag from flying high and following me wherever I go.

Actually, *they* follow me wherever I go. *They're* my stupid freak flag.

But I can't very well go around telling my new friends the truth about them, can I? I can't just announce, "I see dead people," like some kind of female Haley Joel Osment. The kid was a loner in that movie for a reason. And yeah, I guess these days it's cool to be weird and different, but not *that* weird and different. It would be one thing if I read tarot cards and wore a pretty rose quartz on a dainty chain around my neck; that would be passable. That might work.

Talking to the air? No. Definitely not okay to be babbling into the empty aisle, all like, "Oh, hey crazy lady, get off me! And spoiler alert, you're actually one of the dead people. I'll just send you on your way. Go be with Jesus!"

Can I do that right now? Hell to the no.

So that's why I'm about ready to spontaneously combust right here in this padded seat. I should be paying attention to the anthropology lecture. Peters is a campus favorite for a reason, and I actually really like this class if our first lecture was anything to go by.

But there are a lot of dead people hanging around campus. I purposely chose a small liberal arts college in a backwater West Virginian town so that spirits wouldn't bombard me like they do in big cities. Lucky for me, I don't see ancient ghosts, so I wasn't worried about the Civil War history here. It's the recently dead who appear to me. And as it turns out, Hayden College has its fair share. They seriously won't leave me alone now that they've realized I can see them. Even though I'm not talking to them or acknowledging them whatsoever, they sure aren't scared to bombard me.

It's like this: I can see the spirit realm. The ghosties sense that about me and send images to my mind. Sometimes it's moments from their lives, or people they love, regrets they have, but usually, it's random objects that make no difference to me. It rarely makes sense. But they do it all the time regardless of whether I'm busy—like right now, in the middle of class. And oh goodie, I'm supposed to be answering a question.

"Umm, sorry, Dr. Peters, what was the question?" I ask, voice cracking. My face burns as everyone in the classroom, living and dead, turns on me. It's a smallish lecture hall, but all fifty seats are filled. Lucky me.

Peters raises a bushy eyebrow, notices the phone tucked in my palm, and turns to another student. "Mr. Ashton, perhaps you could enlighten us?" The heavy gazes of my classmates turn from me to someone sitting in the back, and I let out a stilted breath. That could have gone better.

A brief silence is followed by a deep silky voice dripping in exasperation. He has a slight accent that for the life of me I can't place. "Anthropology comes from the Greek words anthropos, meaning human, and logos, meaning logic. That's an easy question, Dr. Peters. If people would listen instead of being glued to their phones, perhaps we could all move on to the more interesting bits."

A few students snicker. Shame washes over me,

along with that awful feeling of being the butt of the joke. I can't believe he called me out like that! And it's not like I didn't know the answer. I just didn't hear the question because of this crack-baby ghosty hovering over me—who by the way, is still on my case, sending image after image of prescription medicine bottles. The shame burns up quickly, consumed by anger as I grit my teeth. I continue to tune out the dead lady's hysterics and turn back to glare at the know-it-all in the last row.

I'm stunned at what I find. An icy chill creeps over my body.

Whoever he is, he's glaring right back, his expression venomous, and with eyes so dark, I swear they're black. It's unsettling to the point of making my pulse race. He sees me looking but he doesn't turn away. A jolt of electricity shoots up my spine. His jaw is clenched tight, accentuating the sharp lines of his cheeks and the fullness of his pink lips. I take him in, this man with a face made of daydreams and nightmares. He's the kind of attractive meant for Photoshop and glossy magazine ads, not real life. And from his brazenness, I'd guess the good looks come with a crap load of arrogance. Gross. Also, total eye-roll.

The marker squeaks against the whiteboard as Peters continues the lecture, bringing the class back to focus.

But I don't turn back. Not yet. Instead, I sneer at

the guy who's still openly staring at me with complete and utter disdain. Like, I'm sorry, but what does he want? He's probably used to women fawning over him, but I refuse to be so predictable and lame. I also don't want to be the first of us to break eye contact. It's as if we're playing a game of cat and mouse, but guess what? Cats are my favorite animals. I have two back home. Plus, I have claws. So back off!

Okay, I don't really have claws. I bite the crap out of my nails if we're being honest. But what I'm trying to say is I'm the cat in this scenario—I'm the winner.

He tilts his head, curls his lip, and averts his gaze.

Ha! I knew I was awesome!

Satisfied, I whip back around and resume my attempts to pay attention. I'm here to learn, dang it! The back of my neck heats all throughout the lecture, like a laser beam is being directed right at me. It's even more distracting than the ghosts all up in my business. But I don't turn around again. Not because I'm afraid of the jerk in the back, but because I don't want to give him the satisfaction of knowing he's bothering me. For whatever reason, the hatred between us is instant and mutual. I smile. It's a nice distraction for a haunted girl.

And lo and behold, a half hour later I find him waiting for me after class.

"Mr. Ashton" leans against the wall in the hallway and the moment he sees me, he pushes off it, stalking toward me like a lion about to attack an innocent baby gazelle. Yeah, I am well aware I just went from awesome feline warrior goddess to a baby gazelle.

"What are you doing here?" he demands, the accusatory tone slamming right through me.

I stop, Cora and Macy at my side. All three of us seem to be momentarily blinded by both his attractiveness and that continued brazenness. I blink rapidly, downright baffled by this behavior. It was one thing to challenge me in class, but to wait for me afterward so he can yell at me? Who does that? It only takes a second for that stunned feeling to evaporate into one of indignation.

"Back off," I snap, stepping forward in challenge. I almost can't believe my fearlessness. I've always been so afraid of the bullies, so ashamed of my curse, my self-esteem weakened by something I couldn't change no matter how hard I tried. I let the kids at my old school walk all over me to the point of graduating early and running away. But not today. Not with him. Something about this feels oddly different.

I glare up into his face, voice tight, "I don't even know you."

He scoffs and shakes his head, pointing at me until his index finger pushes against my shoulder. "Don't play dumb. I know what you are."

My whole body lights up with recognition, but not in a good way. I step back, nerves rushing through me like electric currents. He knows *what* I am? He knows I'm a medium? How?

"Don't touch her!" Cora bursts forward, her voice an angry growl. She's the kind of person I wouldn't want to mess with, but he doesn't even give her a second glance.

"This is my territory," he says, leaning in closer, hateful eyes trapping me in.

My inner voice is screaming at me to run far, far away. But something else inside me, something base and primal, wants to destroy him, to tear him limb from limb. Who does he think he is?

Our classmates have begun to form around the two of us, mixed expressions of shock and outrage and curiosity and even delight glued to their prying faces. But nobody intervenes. Go figure.

"Your territory?" I question with a laugh. "What is this, Westside Story? Like I said, I don't even know you. And don't you ever lay a hand on me again."

He pauses for a second, looking me up and down like I'm half diseased, like I smell bad or something. Do I smell bad? I quickly inhale and catch his scent; it's campfire and spice and oddly intoxicating. He's dressed in the kind of laid-back black t-shirt and jeans that cost a fortune to look like he doesn't care about his wardrobe. Typical. I'm wearing butter-soft black leggings and an oversized Gryffindor hoodie. And proud of it! His nostrils flare and that "could cut glass" jaw tenses again.

The moment stretches out between us, taut as a wire. Nobody moves. Nobody speaks. I suddenly grow hot. A ghostly gurgle of water streams across the floor, pooling at our feet an inch thick. I look down and stare, panic rushing through me. *Not now!* It seeps into my high top sneakers. Nobody else sees it. Nobody feels it. Dread sweeps over me. Where did it come from?

"Pack your things and get the hell out of this town," he hisses under his breath, the venom in his tone meant to sting. I blink up at him, out of my element. Then he pushes past me, his broad shoulders nearly knocking me to the tiled floor, into the ghostly water that only I can see.

I'm speechless.

Macy rushes to steady me, her face pale and her wide eyes twinkling with worry. "Are you okay, Hazel? What was that about?"

"I don't know," I croak, confused as ever. Blood rushes to my cheeks as my adrenaline begins to fade, and I realize that everyone is staring at me. Why is this crap always happening? Seriously, I cannot handle another bully, especially one that *looks like that.* Good Lord, he's sexy and scary and I don't even know what to do with this situation.

Cora slides her ebony arm through mine, tugging me close. The water sloshes around my ankles and I refuse to look at it for too long, to search for whatever spirit is doing this to me. Cora's a physically affectionate person in general, and something about her vanilla perfume and warm skin relaxes me a fraction.

I can get through this. With friends like her, I'll be okay.

"Dang girl," she sighs dramatically. "What on earth did you do to piss off Dean Ashton?"

BE SURE TO READ CROWN OF DRAGONS TO FIND OUT WHAT HAPPENS NEXT!

ACKNOWLEDGMENTS

Thank you to everyone who helped me with this fun little novella, from my editor Kate Foster, to my cover designer Ruxandra Tudorica, to my proofreaders: Sarah, Kate, and Ailene. You all rock so hard! And if course the biggest thanks goes out to you, my readers. I couldn't do this without you. If you liked my book, please consider leaving a written review on Amazon or Goodreads and telling your bookish friends.

ABOUT THE AUTHOR

Nina Walker lives in beautiful southern Utah with her family. She writes across multiple genres, hoping to entertain both teens and adults with metaphysical magic systems, forbidden romances, and heart-pounding plot twists. Please visit www.ninawalker-books.com to learn more or follow her shenanigans on Instagram at @ninabelievesinmagic.